THEY CALL ME
ALEXANDRA GASTONE

✧ ✧ ✧

T.A. MACLAGAN

Full Fathom Five Digital is an imprint of Full Fathom Five, LLC

They Call Me Alexandra Gastone

Cover design by Fiona Jayde

ISBN 978-1-63370-060-4

First Edition

To my parents.
For all your love and support through the years.

TABLE OF CONTENTS

TABLE OF CONTENTS

THEY CALL ME ALEXANDRA GASTONE

Prologue

Seven Years Ago

I stared at the video screen. At the girl with my eyes—one blue and one gray-green. I'd seen this video hundreds of times, so I knew it by heart. It was of Alexandra Gastone walking home from school with a friend. I knew every laugh, smile, and eye roll. I knew when she would play with the locket around her neck and when she would swipe a piece of hair behind her ear, twisting it at the end of the motion. I swiped my own newly shorn hair behind my ear, once, twice, three times, always taking care to twist at the end. The action felt natural now. After months of watching the video, it was ingrained. I smiled into the mirror at my side. Alexandra's smile was crooked, and mine now echoed hers, the left side dipping down. I had to strain to keep the smile in place. Seeing a face in the mirror that was not my own jarred me every time. I let the smile fade and brought a hand up to trace my new jaw, studying the stronger angle. I ran a finger down my new nose. It was smaller now, and more refined. The changes might have made me prettier, but I missed my old face. A part of me had been stolen.

I jerked as a cold hand rested on my shoulder.

"What is your name?" asked Mistress.

"Alexandra Gastone," I replied, dropping my voice to match Alexandra's deeper alto.

"What is your age? Who were your parents? Where are you from?"

Unlike many kids who liked to mumble, Alexandra spoke with great elocution, the movements of her mouth a lip reader's dream. "I'm eleven years old," I said, molding my mouth to each word. At Compound Perun, Oline—my native language—had been forbidden within months of my arrival. I now spoke with a perfect American accent. "My parents were Gregory and Tabitha Gastone. I lived in Topeka, Kansas."

"Who is your guardian?"

The video screen went black for a second, and then a different face appeared. It was a new video I hadn't seen, although I recognized the silver hair, weathered face, and intelligent blue eyes. I glanced over at my friend Varos, who controlled the feed. He offered a smile, his chubby face pinched. I could tell Varos was equally as nervous. I wasn't the only one about to embark on a new assignment.

"My grandfather, Albert Gastone," I said, turning back to the video. Back to the man whose life I was about to infiltrate.

"Where does Gastone work? What are his hobbies?"

"He works for the CIA. He's one of the their public liaisons and an analyst specializing in the Southern Caucasus. Albert likes to read, travel, and play strategic games like chess. He has a gun collection."

"When was the last time you saw your grandfather?"

"I was five years old. He was at my birthday party and gave me a chess set."

Mistress squeezed my shoulder. I stifled a shiver as she kissed the top of my head. "Very good, my little silver fox," she said, her icy hands coming to my cheeks. She turned me to the mirror, her face dipping to within millimeters of my own. I could feel the wetness of her breath, smell the stench of vodka. My skin crawled, but I remained still. We gazed at the mirror's reflection. "You must think strategically at all times. Gastone has lived alone for years. It may be hard for him to accept you. Show an interest in his hobbies, and do not disturb his quiet lifestyle. Position yourself as a protégé. Outside of your life with Gastone, you are to assess the strategic value of those you meet. Befriend those of worth, and discard the rest."

"Yes, Mistress."

"Milena Rokva is dead. You are now Alexandra Gastone. Remember that, every second of every day. Albert Gastone may not have seen Alexandra in years, but he will inherit all the photos and videos that have ever been taken of her."

I studied Mistress's cold blue eyes. They were daring me to prove myself. I smiled Alexandra's crooked smile. From deep within, I pulled out a laugh, letting my breath catch almost immediately on it as Alexandra always did, as if shocked by her own amusement. "I'm Alexandra Gastone, the girl next door. I like to play soccer, swim, and read. I like school, and my favorite subject is math." I brushed my hair behind my ear, twisting it at the end of the motion. "I have a crush on a boy named Peter."

Mistress nodded and flicked a hand toward Varos. In response, new images flooded the screen. They were a visual torrent, a deluge to which I'd become well accustomed. The American flag, mansions, fancy cars, fat people living fat lives, money, money, money…the inundation continued driving deep into my psyche…American soldiers in Olissa, their tanks on our streets, their army base on our land. The images flew by…a reel of horrors…and then…without warning, they stopped. The image that remained would echo in my bones, forever and always. My mother—dead, a shot to the head.

In the photo, she lies on the ground, muddy with blood, and I'm next to her, streaked in crimson, hugging a body that life left long ago. My eyes are hollow. Haunted.

I can feel it rush back to me, the crack of the gun, the sound of my mother's body dropping, the warmth of her life seeping away as night fell. One bullet, less than a second, and everything changed. I was broken, and she was gone. A week later, I was at Perun.

The image was a knife carving my insides, but I couldn't look away. It slowly dissolved into the next slide, and I wished the memory of that day would fade as easily. A map of Olissa replaced the shattering photo of my mother.

A small country of ten million, Olissa had suffered centuries of oppression because it was nestled between world titans. On the animated screen, the great country of Olissa began to shrink as it was devoured by powerful neighbors. The video said it all. I served so Olissa would not disappear. So it would not be forgotten. Entranced, I actually flinched when the image vanished, replaced again by the picture of Albert Gastone.

I glanced at Mistress.

"A reminder," said Mistress, "of why you serve. What you are about to do won't be without its trials. Every day you must remember why you do this. Why you fight. It is for Olissa and her people."

"I will remember. For Olissa. Always."

For my mother. Always.

Mistress kissed my cheek and stepped away. "Very good. Now it's time to prepare you for the accident."

Despite my anxiety, I wanted to laugh at Mistress's words. They sounded so casual, like I was simply going to take a bath or pack a bag. I wanted, with all my heart, to serve and honor my mother, but I was still frozen with fear. I'd only just healed from the plastic surgery, and now there would be far more pain. I had to look like a girl who barely survived a car crash. Two men waited outside the door for Mistress's orders. Trying to see past the pain looming, I glanced at the video screen and the man named Albert who would soon believe he was my grandfather. He looked like a good man. His face was gentle and his smile warm. I wondered briefly if he would come to love me but then pushed the idea from my thoughts. His love didn't matter, only his name. It was a name that would get me into a good college and then into the CIA, the very agency where he worked. One day, I would be positioned to pass strategic intel back to Perun.

Varos stood and cleared his throat, drawing our attention. "May I have a word in private with—" Varos looked to me. "With Alexandra. As her handler, I have a few final things to discuss."

"Of course," said Mistress, her words of agreement not matching her heavy scowl. Mistress liked Varos as much as she liked me, which was to say not at all. Seven years my senior, Varos was a chubby asthmatic. Despising physical weakness, Mistress would have loved to crush Varos into shape or watch him perish in the attempt. Fortunately for Varos, he was exceedingly smart with high-ranking parents in the movement. Because of this, he was groomed for an advisory role at Perun instead of an operative position and was kept out of Mistress's clutches. Only eighteen years old, he was about to be the youngest handler and operations leader in the field.

Mistress turned to me before leaving, "For the blood of the fallen. For the blood of the living. For Olissa we fight."

I stood, bringing my hand up in a salute. "For Olissa we fight."

Mistress left without another word, her hard-soled boots tapping out a steady rhythm on the floor.

I turned to Varos as he walked over and our eyes locked. I could feel myself shaking and was trying to regain control. All I wanted to do was race across the room and throw myself into his arms for one last moment of comfort, but I made myself stay rooted in place. To Varos, I was the little sister he never had, someone to watch over and protect, and I…well…I thought of him as more than a brother. I would have shared my fears with him as I'd done so many times over the years, but as my handler, our relationship had to change, become strictly professional. Varos told me so himself. Not friends, not brother and sister, not anything but handler and agent. He would keep his distance in order to remain objective about my performance.

Varos reached me after what seemed like an eternity, time moving slowly but also coming too quickly. Behind the door, a beating awaited. I ran my fingers over the bell-shaped burn on my wrist—one of Mistress's punishments. At Perun, I was no stranger to pain, but I knew those instances were nothing compared to what was only moments away.

Varos put a hand on my shoulder. Unlike Mistress's, his hand was warm. Inviting. He pulled me close and wrapped me in a big bear hug, a hug reserved for me and no one else. I surged with relief he could be my friend for just a few more seconds. "Albert Gastone is a kind man, Little O," said Varos, using my father's nickname for me. "And I'll be there to guide you. You were made for this. You have all the skills you'll need."

The door hinges whined as two of Perun's enforcers entered the room—Negar and Raykom. Raykom was my Sambo instructor, Negar weaponry. I'd never dreamed I would one day face them alone in a room. I'd never dreamed I would be expected to take their hits, offering none of my own in return. They carried several props to aid in their work: straps, a glass window, a two-by-four. My injuries needed to mirror those of a car accident. A bribe to a well-placed doctor would make sure no mention was made of my plastic surgery, but that was as far as a bribe could take me. For the rest of the hospital staff, and for Gastone, my injuries needed to be authentic. There were no shortcuts.

Varos pulled away after kissing my forehead. "For Olissa we fight. For your mother," he said, offering his own salute.

Unable to speak or coordinate my actions, I only nodded in response. The pain was for a greater cause, and because of that, I would bear it with pride and dignity. I would do anything for the cause and for my country. It was an honor. Varos smiled weakly. "See you on the other side, Little O."

I watched each step Varos took in leaving the room. Fifteen in all.

It took Raykom ten steps to reach me. Negar only eight.

1

Old Mr. Dagby grabbed the remote control and turned the volume to blaring. Dagby's hearing aids were acting up again, putting us all at risk for hearing loss.

"Reporting for Edu Channel, I'm Hunter Ludlum coming to you from Olissa, where we have breaking news." Hunter's curly blond hair danced about his head as he stood in front of the Olissan parliament building, the chaos of an angry horde in the background. "The election results for the Olissan presidential race are in, and Vladik Kasarian of the liberal party has narrowly defeated independent candidate and prominent businessman, Tarkan Aroyan. Aroyan and his followers have taken to the streets in protest, claiming election tampering by the United States. Throughout his campaign, Aroyan called for the removal of all US troops on Olissan soil, including the strategically located US army base in Tancred, near the Iranian border."

The camera shifted focus from Hunter to Kasarian's arrival at the parliament building. Instead of a limousine or town car, as you might expect for a politician, he arrived in a black van to accommodate his sister Alina's wheelchair. Flanked by heavy security, he rolled Alina down the van ramp and quickly hustled inside. Hunter flashed back on the screen. "Vladik Kasarian has just arrived and will make his victory speech in only moments. Please stay tuned."

Mr. Dagby switched off the TV. "Can anyone tell me why Aroyan came so close to winning the election?"

The class sat silent for several long seconds, Dagby's question lingering in the air. Half the students averted their eyes, trying not to get called on.

"Anyone?" asked Dagby.

Hating to see him struggle, I raised my hand.

"Yes, Lex!"

"When we saved Olissa from a land grab by Russia and Iran, the United States was seen as a friend, but that was more than a decade ago. We've only increased our troop presence since then. We are now the occupier."

Forty years into teaching, Dagby always had an unsettled look about him. I think he feared his life's work had all been for nothing, we didn't appreciate his efforts, and he hadn't made a difference in our lives. This was a shame because he was by far the best teacher in the high school.

"An occupier? Would you go that far?"

"I may not, but Olissans might. They've had ten years of independence here, and twenty there. For the last five hundred years, every generation has known what it is to be occupied by another nation. It also hasn't helped several American companies operating in Olissa have been busted for fraud. It makes us look bad."

"Some interesting thoughts, Lex," said Dagby, turning his attention to another student. "Mr. Rogan, why do you think Vladik

Kasarian made a point to have his sister Alina at his side during the campaign? She attended every public gathering and was always front and center."

Tim's face went blank. Seconds passed, and I watched as beads of sweat formed on his brow.

"She is confined to a wheelchair—do you think that has anything to do with it?" asked Dagby, trying to help Tim out.

Tim shook his head no.

"She's also a prominent physicist."

Tim nodded hesitantly.

Trying to hide his annoyance, Dagby started to motion for more information just as the end-of-school bell rang, saving Tim from further torment.

With an afterschool appointment to keep, I made a beeline for my locker and began dumping books into my backpack with one hand while checking my phone for a text from Varos with the other. We were more than a week overdue for our monthly meeting, but I still hadn't received a text with the location. Our last meeting had ended poorly, and I was worried Varos might be angry and putting me off. After finding my inbox empty, I stuffed the phone into my bag with everything else and told myself to forget it. Varos still had two more days to make contact before protocol required I reach out directly to Perun.

My boyfriend Grant showed up as I was zipping my bag. The son of a CIA analyst as well as the high school quarterback, Grant provided me with social standing in addition to being another link to the agency. He propped himself up on a closed locker and gave me one of his dimpled smiles, eyes twinkling behind his glasses.

"Wanna hang out?" he asked, reaching over to fiddle with the locket at my neck. "The coach canceled practice for the day since we're all kinda beat up." With his free hand, Grant lifted his shirt a couple of inches to reveal a rather spectacular bruise.

I winced. Grant was an athlete in geek's clothing. Looking at him, you'd never suspect he was the quarterback with the highest pass completion rate in the state. He looked like he'd be more comfortable at a video game arcade than on a football field.

Grant tucked a stray piece of hair behind my ear. "You could come over to my house, and maybe we'd luck into another blackout," he said with a wink.

I laughed. "I'd like to, but I really need to work on Dagby's paper."

"All right. Well, don't forget I'm your ride to school tomorrow."

"Yep, that's cool. I'll see you then." I leaned in to give him a quick kiss, but Grant had a different idea. Taking me into his arms, he dipped me backward, old movie style, and kissed me with skillful intensity. For a few seconds, I melted, caught up in Grant's enthusiasm. Then he lost his balance and dumped me on my butt.

"Oh my God," said Grant, his voice indicating utter mortification. He was sprawled on top of me, his face smushed into what there was of my cleavage. "I'm so sor—"

Grant stopped speaking as I began to shake with laughter. Grant was a romantic, but somehow his efforts never quite materialized as promised. It was a "Grantism" I couldn't help but find charming. My last assigned boyfriend, Kyle "I'm Gorgeous and I Know It" Donovan was all smooth moves and false bravado. I much preferred Grant's more earnest attempts at romance, even if they sometimes left me battered.

Grant rolled to the side and propped himself on an elbow, his smile sheepish.

Still laughing, I tousled his hair. "You're such a doof," I said, pecking his cheek before hauling myself to standing.

"See you later, alligator," said Grant, waving from his place on the floor.

Smiling, I rolled my eyes. "In a while, crocodile."

Thinking of Grant's kiss as I walked to my car, my heart started to flutter—a sensation I wasn't prepared for. It may have ended with us in a heap on the floor, but the beginning started with great promise. Grant had a habit of catching me off guard, and I was flustered by the ferocity of his kiss and the feeling that was obviously behind it. Inside my old Chevy Apache, I leaned back and closed my eyes, allowing myself a moment for thoughts of his lips on mine. Their feel—soft but firm. Their taste—a combination of mint and oranges.

"Close but far, close but far," I muttered, recalling Varos's concern over the relationship.

Spies don't have the liberty of real relationships. You must keep an emotional distance from Grant without him realizing it. Close but far, he'd said.

I shook my head.

His taste…

His feelings…

My…

"Stop it, stop it, stop it." I commanded my thoughts to be silent. "You're being supremely ridiculous."

I focused on my breathing, inhaling long and deep.

One breath…two breaths…three breaths…

After a minute, my thoughts stilled, and I opened my eyes. *Right, time to get going.* I stuck my key in the ignition, said a quick prayer my truck would start, then gave it a turn. The engine coughed twice then sputtered to life. The truck, a 1960s model, was formerly Albert's—as in, he bought it new in the 1960s. Given its senior citizen status, the truck's reliability was questionable at best. I patted the dashboard. "Good boy." Martine was expecting me, and I hated to make her wait.

As I made my way out of the school parking lot, I noted two vehicles that were new to the school grounds with drivers I'd never seen. The first was a non-descript silver Toyota Camry inching out of a parking space, with Virginia tag 777-GN8. The driver was a wide-shouldered, bearded male wearing a plaid shirt. The second was a black Suburban with a female redhead in her mid-thirties, with New York tag 552-NR1. Asa King and Lydia Ogawa had the same Toyota, but their cars had novelty license plate frames. No one at Fair Valley East, neither teacher nor student, had a black Suburban. It was second nature for me to pick out what didn't belong. My years at Perun had taught me threats surrounded us constantly, no matter where we were.

I logged all the information on the cars and the drivers into two mental folders, one for each driver, and watched as both cars fell in line behind me. I closed and filed the folder on the Toyota when it turned left out of the lot and sped off. The redhead turned right and followed me down the road at a respectful distance.

I made a left.

She made a left.

I made a right.

She made a right.

Even when I made a turn for the seedier side of downtown, she continued to follow. Until that point, I hadn't been worried as I was following the standard route into town, but the area I now approached was a total dead zone. I was about to turn down an alleyway to see if she would continue tailing me when she veered into a Burger King.

Another folder closed and filed…

2

I aimed my Kalashnikov at Martine's retreating figure and fired. The bullet caught her in the right leg, and she pitched forward onto the pavement. "Take that, bitch," I yelled. She rolled, bringing her Glock around and firing. I dove behind a dumpster. Her shot went wide.

"You're cheating," said Martine, hitting pause on the game and dropping her controller on the table.

"I am so not," I said, smiling.

"You've played before. There's no way you could be this good on your first time out."

We were an hour into playing *Espionage 4* at The Gamespot, the local gaming parlor, and so far, Martine was losing big time. A self-proclaimed goddess of the video game, she didn't take kindly to being squashed, especially by a gaming serf like me.

Martine grabbed her soda and a handful of chips. "You're really telling me you haven't played this one before?"

"Yes!" I said, nearly yelling. The game was doing an admirable job of simulating the drills I'd been trained in at Perun, which partially accounted for the luck I was having.

"My shots keep going wide. It's like you've got eyes on the back of your head the way you move so quick."

I laughed. "More like I have peripheral vision. You tense before you're about to fire, so I know when to zig out of the way."

Martine's mouth dropped. "You're kidding me, right? You're saying I have a tell, and you can see it out of the corner of your eye with everything going on in front of us?" Martine waved at the high-def screen.

"Yeah, I guess I am saying that," I replied, offering Martine my best aw-shucks smile.

"Well, crap. Let's play something else."

Martine was a senior at Fair Valley West, my school's rival. She was half Chinese, half French, and I'd first met her at The Gamespot. Wanting a temporary reprieve from being Alexandra, I'd come in on a whim after a meeting with Varos. As luck would have it, I sat next to Martine, who saw me go through ten bucks in quarters in less than five minutes trying to play Super Mario Bros. on a vintage machine. Taking pity on me, she offered up some pointers, and a friendship was born.

My social group at Fair Valley East was J. Crew preppy with a little Abercrombie and Fitch mixed in. As Martine didn't fit this mold, I found her immediately refreshing. Martine was Project Runway meets punk. She had eyebrow piercings, fluorescent red hair, and an asymmetrical haircut. She also had a tattoo of a butterfly across her upper back. To compliment her hair, tat, and piercings, Martine liked to wear the best of French fashion. She regularly wore Christian Louboutin, Jean Paul Gaultier, and Frank Mechaly.

Martine and I had bonded over a shared interest in the arts and our lack of parents. Her mom passed away from cancer when she was five, and despite living in downtown DC, Martine's father, a Chinese diplomat, was largely absent from her life, preferring the world of politics over his teenage daughter. Martine lived with her maternal grandmother. I kept Martine on the periphery of my life as Lex Gastone and, because of that, I was able to talk to her about my love of ballet—a hobby the actual Alexandra had failed at and had no interest in.

"So how are things with your quarterback?" asked Martine. "Did you do the deed last weekend like you thought you might?"

"Ah. No," I said, shaking my head and trying not to look guilty. Grant and I had come close over the weekend, but then I'd done my usual and panicked, Varos's words rolling through my mind over and over. *Close but frickin' far.* Then Grant had done his usual post-girlfriend-panic-attack behavior and had acted like the perfect gentleman, suggesting we watch a movie instead. We'd been watching a lot of movies lately.

Martine raised an eyebrow. "Well, why the hell not? From the way you talk about him, he sounds as sweet as can be. You need to put that poor boy out of his misery."

"I don't know why," I said, fiddling with my controller.

"Are you scared?" she asked, her voice serious. "I've never slept with a dude, but I hear it only really hurts the first time and—"

"I'm not scared it'll hurt, it's just the time hasn't been right."

Martine grimaced. "Please tell me you're not one of those girls that wants the fairy-tale first time?" She reached across the couch and took my hand. "Because honey, guys just don't key into that sort of thing. You'll be a virgin for the rest of your life if you're waiting for the fairy-tale princess ending."

I gagged. *Fairy tale? Princess? Me?* "No, I'm not expecting a Cinderella story. Thank. You. Very. Much." Desperately wanting to get off the topic of sex, I switched gears. "Speaking of fairy tales, did I mention Grant and I are up for homecoming king and queen, if you can believe that?"

"Of course I can. You guys are apple pie. Congrats! I'm sure you'll win."

I shrugged. I might not be a princess, but Grant was certainly a prince. "It'll make Grant happy, so that's good. He loves that kind of stuff. How are things with Sadie?"

"We're up for homecoming king and queen, too," said Martine with a smirk and a twinkle in her eye.

I laughed. "Well, that ain't apple pie."

"More like French Silk," she said, winking. "Now, speaking of relationships, have you given any more thought to trying to hook my grams up with your grandpa?"

"I'm not sure he's ready."

"What?" said Martine, her eyes widening. "You said he hasn't been on a date since you came to live with him. How many years ago was that? Like fifteen?"

"Almost seven."

"Jesus, girl. He's old, but that doesn't mean he needs to be a monk. Don't you think my grams is good enough? She's still a real looker."

"Of course I do."

I loved Amélie. Whenever I went over to Martine's, Amélie stuffed me full of dessert and told me stories about being a young girl in France during World War II. She was fascinating and probably someone Albert would love.

"It's just… Why are you pushing this so much? You haven't even met my grandfather. Do you want your grandma out of the house more or something? Maybe so you and Sadie can have some alone time?"

Martine waved a hand in front of her face. "Fa," she said. "The way you talk about your grandfather, he has to be awesome. And Grams loves Sadie. She even suggested I invite her over for another sleepover."

"Really? So you haven't told her yet?"

"I was going to, but then she suggested the sleepover, so I thought I'd wait. I'm thinking I might mention it when I go off to college in the fall. Besides, my father will disown me, and I'm not ready for that. Did I tell you he called the other day?"

I raised an eyebrow and shook my head.

"He asked for a father/daughter date in a few weeks' time. Said he missed me." Martine's voice indicated skepticism.

"Well that's good, right?"

Martine frowned. "Maybe. He asked me to do something about my hair and said no piercings for the night."

I grimaced. Martine was perfect just as she was. I'd never met another teenager so comfortable in her own skin and true to herself. I envied her. "Are you gonna go?"

Martine nodded, but her gaze left me as her thoughts turned internal. For a brief time, her face was clouded with what had to be negative thoughts, judging by the furrowed brow, but then she pulled her focus back into the room. "Grams really wants me to. So yeah, I guess I will." A wry grin spread across her face. "Who knows, last time I saw my dad, he gave me a car. Maybe it's time for an upgrade."

"You have a BMW."

"With gas prices topping six bucks a gallon, I need something economical. Something like a Tesla Roadster. A plug and play." Martine's eyes went dreamy for a moment. "How cool would that be?"

"Aiming high much?" I said, taking a peek at my watch. "I better get going. I'm fixing dinner tonight for my grandpa. It's book club night."

"We still on for our senior ditch day next week?" asked Martine as we headed out.

I nodded, pushing open the door. "Most certainly."

A cold breeze smacked us both in the face as we left The Gamespot. Martine shivered, folding her arms in over her chest. "And what about that big appointment we have for your birthday?"

"Still game for that, too," I said, digging for my car keys.

"Have you thought about what you want?"

"Yep, but you'll just have to wait to find out," I replied, smiling mischievously.

Martine groaned and poked me in the ribs in protest. As I was batting her hand away, I saw the man again, the bearded man in plaid, the driver of the silver Toyota from the school parking lot. Standing at a USPS mail drop box across the street, he was staring directly at me.

3

With Martine around, I could do nothing but watch as the bearded man turned and walked away. By the time I reached my car, he was gone. I spent a half hour scouring the streets for him before having to abandon the task for more conventional pursuits like grocery shopping and making dinner.

The sun was beginning to fade as I pulled into the garage of Albert's farmhouse and parked next to his pride and joy—a silver Jag XKE. The house Albert and I shared was a hundred-year-old beauty built by Albert's own grandfather. It had once sat on a thousand acres of prime Virginia farmland, but now occupied a hundred acres and was flanked by three different McMansion subdivisions. Since Fair Valley was a twenty-minute car ride to downtown DC, land speculators regularly asked Albert to name his price for the remaining land. He had yet to give them a number, which made Albert pretty damn cool in my book.

"Hey, Grandpa," I called out, plopping the grocery bags on the kitchen counter.

"Hey, Lex," answered Albert, coming into the kitchen. He carried a copy of *Mockingjay* by Suzanne Collins, an index finger holding his place. "I expected you back ages ago."

"Sorry. A friend was having calculus troubles so I said I'd help."

"Well that was nice of you."

I shrugged. "I'll have dinner ready in about an hour. That should give you enough time to finish," I said, nodding toward his hand. We alternated who got to pick each week's book, and *The Hunger Games* was mine. Normally, we liked to torture each other. He'd pick old and dry books like *The Art of War*, and I'd pick something with lots of romance or teen angst. With *The Hunger Games*, I'd gone easy on him, thinking he might appreciate the underlying themes, and I'd been right. He'd devoured the first two books and was within spitting distance of finishing the trilogy. If I could settle my feelings of unease about my possible tail, I knew the night's book club would be more fun than most.

"Sounds good," said Albert. "Guess what?"

"We've won the lotto?"

"No," said Albert, rolling his eyes. "But something just as exciting. I've been invited to the gala dinner honoring the Olissan President, Vladik Kasarian. He's scheduled a US trip for talks with President Claymoure."

"That's great," I said, switching on the gas and setting a pot to boil. "I know how much you've been wanting to meet Kasarian."

"But that's not even the best part."

I looked up to find Albert bouncing up and down. He was grinning from ear to ear, and his clear blue eyes glistened with excitement. He looked like a giddy five-year-old the night before Christmas—either that or a man who really had to pee. I couldn't help smiling.

"What's the best part?"

"You're my plus one."

I nearly dropped my can of tomatoes. Unable to find my words, I grabbed a few more items from the grocery bag and set them on the counter to buy some time.

"So. What do you think?" asked Albert.

"Wow, Grandpa. Are you sure you want to take me and not a real date? What about one of those ladies I introduced you to at church?"

"Nonsense, girl. You've already had a background check. Taking someone else would just be a pain. Don't worry. You'll love it. There will be tons of interesting people to chat up. Vladik's sister, Alina, will be there. She seems like a particularly interesting young lady to meet."

I walked around the counter to give Albert a hug. "I can't wait."

Albert patted my back. "Give me a holler when supper's ready."

I watched him retreat to the living room. For a seventy-year-old man, he was in remarkably good shape. His posture was strong, he was visibly muscular, and he still moved with ease. His mind had also stayed sharp, perhaps because he'd refused to retire and still made daily trips into his office at the CIA. The Gastones had good genes. Most of the clan lived well into their nineties, and I often wondered if I would make it half as long living as an impostor. Although I liked the idea of living to a ripe old age and taking up hobbies like shuffleboard and croquet, I knew spies didn't have a long shelf life and had come to terms with that reality. I was willing to trade old age for the safety of Olissa. A retirement enclave down in Boca was not in my cards.

For the blood of the fallen. For the blood of the living. For Olissa we fight.

I returned to cooking, wondering what the faces in my locket photos would be doing now if they had survived the car crash. Alexandra's father, Greg, had been a special agent for the FBI. Like a policeman's son becoming a fireman, Greg had joined the FBI in a fit of rebellion against his CIA father during their estrangement. I figured Greg would still be at the FBI, but he and Albert would have reconciled. Albert refused to go into details about the rift, but I couldn't fathom anyone staying mad at Albert. Tabitha, a stay-at-home mom, would have popped out a few more kids. She had grown up in foster care, bouncing from home to home, and had wanted a big family to make up for what she'd missed out on growing up.

As I continued prepping dinner, I stifled thoughts of Tabitha and Gregory. Thinking of them helped keep me in character as their orphaned daughter, but if I thought of them too often or for too long, I lost my perspective and my edge. I started to feel guilty they had died, and at Perun, I'd learned guilt was something a good spy couldn't afford. Gregory and Tabitha were Perun's casualties, sacrificed for the cause. I also couldn't let my concern over the bearded man change my behavior around Albert. I needed to be "on" all the time. So I poured all my concentration into making the best meal possible.

"Grandpa, dinner's ready!" I called out some time later as I drizzled homemade walnut oil dressing over the spinach side salad. I popped a crouton slathered with the dressing into my mouth and tasted the very distinct, rich nuttiness of the oil then licked my fingers clean. It was perfect.

Book club night meant we dined in style. Instead of Corelle at the table in the kitchen alcove, we ate on Albert's wedding china at the antique cherry table in the dining room. We even sipped our sodas out of crystal glasses. Albert didn't have one fancy bone in his body, but Fern, his late wife, did, and I think using the china and crystal made him feel connected and loyal to her, a trait I found endearing as she'd been dead for over thirty years.

I took the plates to the table and sat. Albert joined me with all three Hunger Games books in hand, and Orkney, my three-legged Scottish deerhound, made his first appearance of the evening. Ork had the uncanny ability of showing up just as food was being served. He laid his snout on my lap, his brown eyes peering up at me hopefully. I patted his head and pulled a dog biscuit from my pocket to tide him over until it was time to lick the plates.

"So," said Albert. "Before we talk books, I want to discuss the upcoming event."

"Kasarian's dinner?"

"No, the other, more important event. Your eighteenth birthday."

"I don't want a party, Grandpa," I said, twirling my spaghetti with a fork.

Albert shook his head. "You've never wanted a party. I think that's abnormal for a teenage girl."

I eyed Albert circumspectly. He was twirling his spaghetti just as I had, something he rarely did. Seeing it put me on edge. Normally, Albert would cut his spaghetti a couple of times and then rotate the plate to get the strands from different angles. Albert approached this routine with the focus of a heart surgeon about to operate. Twirling his spaghetti meant Albert was preoccupied. If I wasn't careful, I was going to end up with a surprise party like the one Albert had thrown when I was twelve. Unsure of who my friends were, he'd invited my whole grade and erected a mini-carnival in the backyard, complete with Ferris wheel and cotton candy vendors. I'd plastered a smile on my face but hadn't enjoyed myself. It wasn't my birthday, after all. Most of the time, it was easy to be Alexandra, but for some reason, on her birthday, it became a lot harder. The burden of the lie was somehow greater on that day. "How about you take Grant and me out to dinner? Someplace fancy in the city like Tosca or Dorian and Gray's and then maybe we could go to a movie afterward?"

Albert nodded. "Good idea. Thanks for throwing me a bone, Lex. Appreciate it."

I smiled. "No problem, Gramps."

Albert devoured a forkful of spaghetti and then patted the books on the table. "Wonderful. Wonderful. Wonderful. I'm so glad you didn't subject me to another one of those bodice rippers of yours."

I laughed. "Figured you needed a break from quivering members and thought you'd like the book's Big Brother and government control themes, given your interest in the Caucasus."

"I did. I did," said Albert. "I loved Katniss. She showed such strength and independence in the books. She reminds me of you."

I waved away the compliment, my stomach doing a few guilty flip-flops. "I liked how Collins blended all the serious themes with a reality show vibe. I think it makes the books appeal to a wider audience."

"The author must have been inspired by the Greek myth of Theseus. Maybe that will be my next choice for book club night. In it, Athens is forced to send offerings in the form of children to Crete, where the children are eaten by a Minotaur."

We spent the rest of dinner going over character motivations and contemplating the parallels with current-day situations. For a book club night, it was enjoyable, and I had, for the most part, been able to keep thoughts of the bearded man at bay. While Albert washed the dishes, I grabbed Ork and headed out for our walk.

Ork was the one constant in my life I felt I could count on, and he had been my anchor since the day I rescued him. It was right after the crash, and I'd just met Albert. Wanting some sort of neutral ground for us, Albert had whisked me away to the Orkney Islands in northern Scotland. It was there I fished a three-legged puppy out of the rough Whitehall surf. Orkney was barely four months old and shook like a leaf after the rescue. His outward display of fear was how I felt on the inside, and I instantly sympathized. Albert must have seen our bond because he had Orkney checked by a vet and made arrangements for his transportation back to the States.

Reaching the dog park at the intersection of two nearby subdivisions, I let Orkney off his leash and watched as he bounded away after a beagle named Maude, his doggie girlfriend. The two of them playing looked like David and Goliath, Maude weaving in and out of Ork's three legs. I headed over to the bench where Maude's owner, Eric, was madly gaming on his phone. "Hey," I said, hunkering down in my seat. "How's it going?"

"Fine, I guess," said Eric, not even glancing up.

Someone else might have been offended by Eric's brush-off, but not me. He could be rude all he wanted as long as he stayed put and gave me the five minutes I needed to mirror his phone. I shimmied closer to Eric and hit the start button on my modified phone so it would begin the syncing process. I'd recently heard some rumors about Eric that needed confirming.

With Fair Valley so close to downtown DC, the area was ideal for families of government officials and those in the CIA, FBI, and NSA. Perun was betting some of my classmates would follow in their parents' footsteps and might be of use someday. In the future, if I needed a favor, I could call upon the dirt I'd acquired via after-hours locker searches and some rudimentary computer hacking. I was after the material on Eric's phone for just such a dirt-finding expedition. Although Eric's family was of little strategic importance to Perun, and the boy himself planned to be a regular old doctor like his dad, if the note I'd found lodged in one of my classmate's books was accurate, Eric was getting paid to take the SATs for other people. Few people escaped their teen years without dirty skeletons, and proof of a foray into standardized test fraud might be just the leverage Perun needed in the future. A test fraud scandal implying low moral character simply wouldn't do for a future senator or congressperson, after all.

While waiting for my phone to complete the sync, I watched Maude and Ork nose an abandoned tennis ball back and forth. Deciding they needed some human participation in their game, they bustled over to our bench, Maude dropping the ball at Eric's feet. When Eric ignored her, she began to whine. Ork turned his attention from Maude to me as if to say, "Well, what are you going to do about this?" My phone pinged twice, indicating it had finished. Mission complete.

"I gotcha, Maude," I said, snatching up the slobber-logged ball. Both dogs began to pant in anticipation. I turned and threw the ball behind the bench. The area was used less frequently by the dogs, and therefore, had more grass on it. If I was going to be playing fetch, I preferred to only deal with the slobber, not the slobber-and-mud combo. As the ball was arcing through the air, I caught sight of a silver Toyota Camry parked on the street. The car was parked close enough I could see someone was inside but far enough away I couldn't define any features or make out the license plate.

In order to get closer without spooking the driver, I began to wave my arms at the dogs. "Come here guys, let me throw it again," I yelled as I moved forward across the park. Ork brought the ball over, and I threw it again, making my way toward the street. I was keeping the car in my peripheral vision. When Maude returned with the ball after my second throw, I chucked the ball toward the road at an angle. It sailed over the fence and into the street. To someone watching, it would look like I merely overshot my mark. "Oh crap," I said, leaning over to pat Ork on the head. "My bad, I'll go get it." I caught Eric's wave as he whistled to Maude and moved toward the far gate. Maude gave Ork a farewell bark and veered off to follow. Perfect.

Now that I was closer to the Camry, I knew it was the same car from school because of the license plate. Catching me off guard, however, was that the person inside wasn't the bearded man in plaid. It was another dude, equally big but with blond hair.

I hopped the fence and jogged over to the ball, which was twenty feet from the car. At my nearness, the man pulled out a map and made like he was lost. *Nice try buddy. Ever heard of GPS?*

Having retrieved the ball, I walked toward the car like I was making my way to the dog park gate. When I was close enough, I heaved the ball back over the fence to Ork, then made a dash for the car.

Two seconds after tossing the ball, my hand found and pulled the Camry's door handle. The driver gasped in surprise and tried to shove me out of the way.

"Why am I being followed?" I said, grabbing his hand and yanking back a finger. I kept my voice low so as not to draw the attention of nearby residents.

"Jesus Christ," said the man, grabbing for something with his free hand. I caught sight of a gun barrel. At seeing it, I pulled the hand I held as far out of the car as I could then slammed the door on his arm. The gun fell from his other hand as he howled in pain.

Acting with surprising mental clarity given the pain he had to be in, the man heaved his full weight against the car door, sending it flying open in my direction. It caught me on my left side and sent me reeling backward. I landed with a thud on the sidewalk, searing pain corkscrewing through my shoulder and down my arm.

"Bitch," spat the driver, reaching across to slam the car door with his uninjured hand. Despite the blazing pain in my shoulder, I somehow staggered to my feet. The engine thrummed to life as I went for the door again. I watched helplessly as the car peeled away from the curb. Not only did I have a tail, but judging from the use of the same car by different guys, they were taking shifts. Something was wrong. Very, very wrong.

With the car out of sight, I turned my attention to my shoulder and found it knobby and distorted. The throbbing was so intense and unrelenting I couldn't move it more than a few millimeters. The car door had hit me in just the right spot to dislocate it. As a blackness began creeping into my vision, I stumbled toward the nearest mailbox and slammed my shoulder against the post to pop it back into place. The pain on impact was of the take-your-breath-away sort, but then it subsided into a dull ache. I sank down onto the sidewalk to catch my breath and steady my nerves. Rubbing my shoulder, I gazed across the street at one of the McMansions. It was in foreclosure, the tailored gardens in disarray. For some reason, my eyes locked onto a scrubby patch of gold chrysanthemums.

"I have a tail," I mumbled.

Part of me still couldn't believe it.

4

_____

"I'm back, Grandpa," I called out, undoing Ork's leash. With a stiff gait, he headed off to his dog bed. My boy was getting old.

"You want to finish losing our game of chess?" asked Albert, coming into the den and nodding toward the board with a wicked grin.

I gave Albert my death glare, but this only made his grin wider and more fiendish.

I'd made a dumb move during our last session of play, and Albert had me cornered. Hating to lose, I was stalling on the game, hoping I'd see a way out. After the dog park, I was wishing I could hit pause on my life as easily as I could on the game.

"I need to work on Dagby's paper," I said with a huff. I had a five-page paper on political secrets due in a little over a week. In it, I was supposed to take some point in history when a secret was kept from the public and critically evaluate how things might have unfolded if the secret had been known at the time. When he heard of the assignment, Albert had challenged me to uncover a secret being kept by Tarkan Aroyan, a.k.a. the man who'd just lost the Olissan presidential race. My interest piqued and as someone who was a glutton for punishment, I'd accepted the challenge. "Care to give me a hint before I take another crack at it?" The paper was of little interest to me after the encounter I'd just had, but I still needed to play my role with Albert.

"The answer is written plain as day, in black and white," said Albert, smiling. "It's out there for everyone to see." He chuckled.

I shot Albert another disgusted look. "Plain as day? Black and white? Can you be more obtuse?"

"I'm sure I could be if I tried," said Albert, winking. "But I'm going easy on you."

Despite all that was going on, I couldn't help but laugh and shake my head. "Good night, Gramps," I said, leaning in to kiss his cheek.

"Love you," replied Albert.

Taken by surprise at his words, I wrapped my arms around him. Albert rarely verbalized his affections, and given the circumstances, that was something for which I was thankful. "You're wonderful, Grandpa," I said, squeezing him tight, hoping the hug would somehow make up for my absent words.

We patted each other's backs and then stepped apart to stand awkwardly, both aware of the elephant in the room. It had been almost seven years, and I still couldn't bring myself to say three simple little words. Or write them for that matter. I'd rehearsed them many times, running through scenarios in my head, but for some reason, they never materialized when needed.

Albert cleared his throat, "Well then, see you in the morning."

"Yeah, see ya," I said, walking to the stairs and taking them two at a time.

As I reached my room, my cell phone buzzed with an incoming text. Hoping it was Varos with an explanation for the tail, I dove inside my bag for the phone. For safety sake, Varos's messages were always in code. They were usually coupon deals or doctor's appointments. The numbers on the message plus two hours indicated the meet time, and the fourth word of the message indicated one of our five standard meet locations.

My heart dipped a little at seeing the message. It was from Perun, but not Varos. The screen showed no words, only a bunch of jumbled letters. To an untrained eye, it would look like an accidental text, maybe one sent by a young kid, but it was really a modified Caesar cipher. In a normal Caesar, the alphabet is shifted a certain number of places to the left or right. For example, in a left shift Caesar of three places, an *A* in the actual text becomes an *X* in the cipher text, a *B* becomes a *Y*, and so on. In Perun's version of the Caesar, the size of the left alphabetical shift changed for each letter of the text, following the pattern of three, five, eight, one, six, then rinse and repeat. The numbers zero through nine were also shifted in the same manner.

I sat down on my bed and began to unscramble the message in my head, hoping it would explain the tail. The message was short and to the point.

> *Handler Replacement. Operative initiation. Meet orchid house. Wednesday 0930.*

The cold and calculating spy in me was relieved to see the message because it accounted for the tail. Something had happened with Varos, and Perun was checking on his operatives. Then there was the other part of me—the non-spy part—that was crazy worried for my old friend. Had Varos been made, or worse, captured? Were they worried he'd given up his operatives? Is that why they were tailing me?

"Why now?" I blurted. I wanted more information. I wanted the novella of texts. The scheduled meet was in a little over twelve hours, and I was being initiated! The plan had been for my activation when I reached the CIA, not before. Whatever was going on with Varos, I doubted they were calling me up for that reason. As a high school student, I wasn't in any position to help him. Then it hit me.

I was Albert's plus one for Kasarian's gala.

From his dog bed, Ork looked up from gnawing at his bone. I glanced at him, then back at the screen, then to him again. I felt a tidal wave of anxiety at all the unknown factors. During our last couple of meetings, Varos's appearance had been disheveled. He'd grown a beard, and his clothes sagged. I'd chalked the change up to a busy work schedule, but then his behavior had also been odd. He'd asked strange questions, and there was the awkward exchange that ended with my own embarrassing freak-out. I'd thought it was some sort of test. Was there more to it than that? And what would be my mission at the gala? Would it be a one and done or the beginning of something long term?

I closed my eyes, took a deep breath, and then opened them to stare at the text again with its mess of letters. It was sooner than I had expected, but my time had come. I was finally being asked to take an active part in helping my country. "It's starting."

Sensing my nervousness, Ork began to whine. He came over to me, and I patted his head absently, my own mind going every which way but straight. "It's okay. Varos will be okay. Whatever happened,

Perun will fix it. They have to, right? He's one of their best."

Ork lifted one of his brows and increased the volume of his whining.

"Someone probably made him, and he's going to be reassigned. That's not so bad," I said, trying to talk myself into believing my words. The thought of navigating my life as Lex without Varos was a kick to the gut. Although more my boss than a friend now, I still cared about him. Probably more than I should. I still saw elements of the boy I'd fallen in love with. Plus, he was the only one in my life who knew the real me. And there was more than that, too. He was my link to Olissa. To home. His presence reminded me of the other cadets who'd become my family, cadets who now served for the good of Olissa, just as I did. Something happening to Varos was a stark reminder of what could happen to any of us. Spying is a dangerous game. "As long as he's safe. That's what matters."

A glass-half-full kind of dog, Ork barked his agreement.

"Now. It's happening now." *Thud, thud, thud* went my heart. I smiled and then frowned and then smiled again. "Now's the time."

I deleted the text and chucked my phone onto the bed. With the mystery of my tail solved, I knew I should get to work on Dagby's paper, but I felt too hyped up to tackle it. The paper was going to have to take a backseat. I had big things on the horizon. Big, scary things. I squared my shoulders and took a deep breath. "Now's the time."

Ork alternated between panting and whining as I grabbed my pajamas and headed for my bathroom. In the shower, I stood under near-scalding water for twenty minutes, fixating on my wrist's bell-shaped scar. I traced its outline over and over, thinking back to who had put it there. My country had suffered so much. Was I finally going to be of use to them?

When my fingertips had turned to prunes, I got out to brush my teeth. After clearing the steam with my hand, I looked at the mirror as I brushed. A five foot ten lanky brunette with straight hair gazed back—one eye blue, one gray-green. Her cheeks were flushed from the heat of the shower, highlighting her high cheekbones and strong jaw.

"Who the hell are you?" I asked the mirror. It was a game I'd played when I first came to live with Albert, a game I hadn't played in years.

The lanky brunette in the mirror blinked several times then spit out a mouthful of toothpaste. "Who do you want me to be?"

I wanted to stop playing the game, but somehow, I couldn't pull my eyes away from the mirror. I watched as Mirror Girl filled a cup with water, took a swig, swished it about, and then spit again before dropping the toothbrush back into its holder.

I searched for an answer to her question, but try as I might, I couldn't find one. "I don't know," I replied, feeling bile rise in my throat. "Who do you want to be?"

Mirror Girl shrugged and reached a hand toward my cheek. "It doesn't matter what I want. It never has."

I studied her eyes, the contrasting orbs. I was trying to see into her soul, but as in the past, she wouldn't let me in. She was a locked vault, and I had no access. Lacking the true core, I was only a façade.

"No, I guess it doesn't," I said, feeling my anger rise.

I wasn't Alexandra, but I also wasn't myself. The image in the mirror was not mine. Recalling a photo of my mother at the same age, I could see none of her in my reflection. Too much of my true appearance had been lost to a surgeon's scalpel, and for the first time, I felt the loss of that connection to my mother—the connection of my heritage. All that was there was the veneer of a dead girl.

A girl I'd never spoken with.

A girl I didn't know.

Feeling another wave of bile rise, I padded over to my bed and crawled under the covers despite being far from sleepy.

Even with the lights off, my room wasn't dark. The moon's light streamed through the wispy, white curtains at my window, creating a dappled pattern on my floor and illuminating the pictures on my nightstand. In one of the images, I was at the Radiohead concert with Grant. In another, at the Great Wall of China with Albert. I picked up the frame with Alexandra and her parents at the zoo, a giraffe in the background. Her tiny hands gripped an ice cream cone, and her face was covered in chocolate goo.

"Who are you?"

Her eyes, one blue and one gray-green, were fixed intently on her ice cream cone. She ignored the camera and my question.

I asked it again. "Who are you, Gastone?" I hadn't asked these questions in years, but now that things were beginning, I felt I needed to know. I somehow owed it to Alexandra.

Ork dropped his bone and looked up at me with a low, guttural whine.

"It's okay," I said, popping the frame back onto the nightstand. "I promise I'm not going crazy."

I spent the next two hours listening to Ork's breathing, willing it to lull me to sleep. Finally, I turned to my dresser and considered the phone. I reached for it then pulled back as Varos's words played through my head. *Close but far. Close but far. Close but far.* Damn you, Varos. For getting made? For getting caught? For telling me to be close but frickin' far and then not being here to help me.

I closed my eyes again, but neither my mind nor my heart was quiet enough for sleep. Varos was missing, and I was being activated. Things were about to change.

I reached for the phone again and snatched it up, moving fast so Varos's words couldn't stop me. Grant picked up on the second ring with a "Hey."

I heard a smile behind his simple greeting and shimmied down into my covers to get comfortable, tucking the phone closer to my ear.

"Hey."

"You having trouble sleeping again?"

"Yeah."

"You want to talk about anything?"

My handler was MIA and I was about to be activated. I wanted to talk about everything, but I could share none of it, not even a morsel. "No, not really. I just want to turn off my brain and stop thinking for a little bit."

"So you called me?" said Grant, feigning offense. "Because I'm the boy toy you keep around for his hot bod and skills in the boudoir?"

"You know it," I said, laughing. "I'm a sucker for boys who are black and blue."

"Yeah, that's what I thought. It's okay. I don't mind being used for my body. I'm game anytime, in fact." Grant paused, then laughed nervously. "No pressure though... Hey, do you want me to tell you another story to help you sleep?"

I nodded and mumbled something that vaguely sounded like a "yes, please" as I closed my eyes. Moments later, Grant's rich story-telling voice found my ear, its tone and cadence my own personal tonic. I immediately felt the sweep of relaxation.

"A long time ago, in a galaxy far, far away…"

5

I woke up to the obnoxious blare of my alarm at six a.m. I clicked it off with a grunt and then rolled over to ponder my ceiling. When I was twelve, I'd stuck a bunch of glow-in-the-dark stars up in the shapes of various constellations, and despite being too old for it now, I still hadn't taken them down.

I stood up on my bed and began to pry the stars loose, taking down both plaster and paint. Ork stared at me and offered the occasional worried sigh. I'd received the stars as a birthday present from Albert one year and had used them as an excuse to act like a real kid for a few hours in the privacy of my own room. Before Perun, stargazing had been one of my favorite hobbies alongside ballet, and in that afternoon, I took great pains to arrange the stars in the formations of actual constellations. When I finished hanging the stars, I'd danced about my room on half point, letting muscle memory guide me into the arabesques and pirouettes my grandmother had taught me. Tchaikovsky's music played in my head, taking me into each new movement as if by magic. For those few hours, I was Milena, not Alexandra, and sometimes at night when I looked up at the stars, I was her again. Although I never danced another step of ballet, looking at the constellations reminded me of what I once aspired to be—a figure of strength and grace. Someone who spoke truth through movements.

But the time for childish endeavors was gone. In fact, it had never truly existed for me, and I chastised myself for pretending it had. Milena was long dead, and a few plastic stars and daydreams about being a ballerina weren't going to change that. Besides, I was something far more important than a ballerina. I was a spy. What I did for my country mattered. It wasn't art. It was life and death.

I took out jeans and a sweater from my closet and laid them on my bed, then went back and grabbed a second set of clothes: my black leather skirt, a white silk blouse, a silk scarf from my summer trip to China with Albert, a pair of knee-high black leather boots, and a black Coach purse. I packed this outfit, the one I planned to wear to my Perun meet, into the Nike duffle bag I used for cheerleading. With the meet during school hours, I was going to have to skip for the day, which was made more difficult by Grant driving me to school.

Grant drove me to school most days as he was heavily into being green. While I appreciated his environmental awareness and his wanting to spend time with me, his desire to carpool sometimes made my life more complicated than it needed to be.

In order to make the meet, I could feign illness with both Grant and Albert, but then I ran the risk of Albert deciding to stay home with me, something that was not out of character. I could tell only Grant I was sick, but then I risked him talking about it in front of Albert. This was a mistake I'd made in the past and didn't want to repeat. Plus, Albert would wonder why Grant didn't pick me up, and I would have to tell another lie. Given the circumstances, I'd decided my best bet was to go to school and then leave—

texting Grant an excuse and telling Albert I'd come home sick. It would decrease the number of lies told and allow me to keep my story simple.

Dressed and ready, I went into the bathroom to grab the one final thing I needed for the day. I pulled open my bottom vanity drawer and took out the box of tampons. Within weeks of coming to live with Albert, I'd put a false bottom in the drawer. Feminine hygiene products equaled a "no-go" zone for Albert and, therefore, made the perfect items for storage in my special drawer. Popping out the false bottom, I retrieved a 4.8-inch plain edge knife by Boker and its sheath and fastened it to my calf before heading to the kitchen.

"Mornin', Lex!" sang Albert as I strolled in and hopped up on one of the stools at the breakfast bar. "I saw you had your lights out early last night. Did you figure out the secret?"

I shook my head. "I got hit with a terrible headache. I've still got a fair amount of time before it's due. I'll attack it this weekend."

"You feeling better?" asked Albert, handing me a plate of French toast.

"It was nothing a good night's sleep couldn't cure. Busy day at work?" I asked.

The doorbell rang just as Albert was about to reply. We both looked at our watches. It was 7:45 a.m. on the dot. "Ah, Grant's here bright and early."

I nodded, a half smile creeping onto my face. While my other classmates made a game out of arriving fashionably late, Grant was nothing if not punctual.

"I'll go let him in," said Albert. "You just finish your breakfast."

I took another forkful of French toast and listened as Albert walked to the front door. "Hey, Grant," said Albert. "How're you doing?"

"Good, sir. And yourself?"

"Oh just fine. There's a big diplomatic dinner coming up I'm pretty excited about. Has your dad mentioned it?"

"Oh yeah. He's very excited to meet Kasarian." Grant's voice dropped, and I had to stop eating to hear what was said. I missed the first part, but caught the last. "Do you know what Lex might want to do for her birthday?"

Hearing that, I gave Ork my plate and headed for the door.

Grant and Albert fell silent as I entered the hall. "I'm ready," I said, grabbing my two bags.

Before Grant could offer to take my bags, I shuffled past him, but I caught a glimpse of him mouthing, *I'll call you later.* Albert nodded in reply.

What is it with people and birthdays? I wondered. Your own birth wasn't an occasion you remembered, and it seemed more like a day you should be giving your parents gifts. After all, they were the ones responsible for your existence. Since I didn't have any parents, either as Alexandra or Milena, I just wanted to forget the whole thing.

Grant edged past me as we neared the car and opened the passenger side door of his charcoal gray Prius. "Thanks," I said, piling in with my bags.

Grant smiled, flashing his dimples, then nudged his glasses into place with the back of his hand. I looked up at his adorable face and felt my throat tighten, my stomach plummet. What would become of the relationship now that I was being activated?

I'd been so focused on being called to serve early and worried about Varos, I hadn't thought about what it might mean for the other aspects of my life.

Despite being annoyed at all the birthday nonsense, I liked being around Grant. My life was better because he was in it. I managed a weak smile before ducking my eyes and pretending to need something out of my backpack. I unzipped the front pouch. "Better get going," I said, fiddling with the contents inside.

Stay focused. You don't know what's going to happen.

Grant started the Prius with a press of a button. "You should ask your grandpa for one of these for your birthday. I know it's a classic, but that Apache of yours is a hog. Something like this would save you a ton of money, especially since the Middle East isn't going to get its act together anytime soon."

"Babe, will you please just drop all the birthday talk. I know that's what you were talking to my grandfather about. I don't like it when people make a big deal out of it. So please don't." I took Grant's hand and squeezed it, in part to drive home that I wanted this birthday business dropped, but also to feel the reassuring warmth of him. I sensed the first hint of nerves hitting at the day laid out before me.

Grant squeezed my hand briefly before pulling onto the road. "You helped make my birthday special with the concert tickets. I know you stood in line all day for those puppies. I just want to do something special for you."

I looked over at Grant as he was driving, studying the kindness in his face, the cute upturn of his mouth that was always there, even if he wasn't smiling. The beautiful green eyes peering out from behind his glasses, always aware and attentive. I wondered if anyone had a better boyfriend. I wondered how it would be if I didn't have to pretend all the time. If I wasn't always scared of losing myself.

"If you want to give me what I want for my birthday, then you'll drop it. Okay?" I replied, my voice a mix of pleading and prickly.

"I don't understand. Everyone likes their birthday." He paused. "At least until they get really old and start worrying about their looks. What gives, birthday scrooge?" Grant chuckled at his little literary joke.

"Because my mom always made a big deal out of my birthday and she's not here to celebrate. And it sucks."

"Shit," said Grant, his face going ashen. "Lex, I'm sorry."

"Look Grant, I slept like crap last night. Can we just drop the whole thing and talk about something more fun… Why don't you tell me about the plan coach has for the homecoming game?"

Grant nodded but still looked pained. His mother had been fighting cancer when I'd met him in middle school. Back then, he'd been a shy, gangly kid with no friends. After nearly a five-year battle, she'd finally died a year and a half ago. His feelings about her loss were still very raw, and by mentioning a lost parent, I was bringing them to the surface. I knew it would stop all talk of my birthday. It didn't even matter I wasn't talking about Tabitha Gastone.

"Why don't we talk colleges instead?" offered Grant. "Did you talk to the Princeton interviewer yet?"

I stared out the front windshield, suddenly dumbstruck. We'd only been in the car a few minutes, and already my emotions were pingponging all over the place. Would there be a Princeton? Would that still be part of the Perun plan? Princeton was Albert's alma mater, and I'd already gone for a visit and had loved it. The gothic architecture was gorgeous, and it seemed like the perfect place to spend four years of college. I'd actually let myself feel excited about going there, but what if none of it was going to happen?

What if the mission was a one-way ticket out of my life as Alexandra?

What if Varos was wrong about my skills?

What if I wasn't up to the task and messed up the mission?

What if I was outed?

There'd be jail.

Torture.

Grant nudged my shoulder, "Lex?"

I turned to him, trying to reel in the thoughts that were spinning out of control. "What'd you say?"

Grant glanced from the road with a look of concern. "The Princeton interview? Did you have it?"

"Yeah, yesterday morning."

"And?"

"Knocked it out of the park," I said, somehow finding a smile. "What about you?"

"Denison didn't go well. The interviewer was an old linebacker—massive guy. He took one look at me and I could tell he wasn't interested. The one with the Chicago rep went pretty awesome, though. He said I should expect an invitation to visit the campus and see the football facilities. I just wish I'd get an invitation from Penn. That would be like a dream. They're a great team, and I'd only be an hour away from you at Princeton…"

My heart caught at hearing Grant's words of hope for our future. It was the first time he'd mentioned wanting to go to a college near to me. We'd been skirting around the issue. If he was only an hour away, we might have a shot at making things work but…

The repercussions of the previous night's message were finally being driven home. The old plan could be completely thrown out the window. The life I'd known for the past seven years could change in an instant, transform into something complicated but also meaningful. I told myself to hold onto that fact. I served for Olissa, and it was an honor.

Even if it meant giving up Grant and Princeton, it would be good to have real work to do. Cultivating potential assets and digging up dirt on people was all well and good, but it wasn't being active. I told myself I was ready for whatever Perun gave me. I told myself this over and over until it finally began to sink in.

I had the skills.

I could do whatever they asked.

For the blood of the fallen, for the blood of the living, I would do whatever they asked.

6

————————

"Lex, are we all right?"

We'd just arrived at my locker and I was still submerged deep in my own head, but somehow I registered Grant's words. Perhaps it was the worry in them that broke through my daze.

I glanced at Grant and found lines of fear and concern written on his forehead. I took his hand and squeezed it. I hadn't seen those lines since his mother's death, and I didn't want them taking hold. "Yeah, of course we are."

"It's just that you've been acting kinda odd. Zoning in and out. Pulling me close and then pushing me away. I didn't know you felt that way about your birthday."

I stopped Grant's words with a kiss and pulled his hand to the small of my back.

Then I froze.

I hadn't intended to, but something in my subconscious yanked me to a halt. Something deep down told me I shouldn't be drawing Grant any closer. It wasn't fair to him. I didn't know what the day would bring.

I pulled free from the kiss and abruptly stepped back. "It's not you. I promise. It's the whole birthday thing and then the college thing," I said, trying to cover for my crazy behavior. I could feel my muscles coiling tight with the tension of the situation. The whiplash of it. "I'm just stressed."

Grant shook his head and pulled me back to him. "No," he said firmly, grabbing my eyes with his. "Not this time."

I wanted to protest. Who was he to say no? But the green expanse of his eyes kept me silent. Captivated. I felt myself begin to fall—fall into him, fall down, fall apart.

Grant leaned down to kiss me again. Only when his lips met mine did our eyes finally close. The kiss wasn't one of our pecks or one of Grant's great shows of affection. It was soft, his lips gently caressing my own, questioning me. *Why do you pull away? Why won't you let me in? What happened to make you like this? Can I help you? Would you let me help you? Heal you?*

He brought a hand to my face and gently cradled my cheek. He wrapped his other hand farther around my back, sparking goose bumps that raced to my fingers and toes. The tension I held began to fade. Evaporate. I forgot the need to push away and sunk into him, folding into his contour. His kiss was filled with such sweetness, I selfishly wanted to take it all in. I wanted the memory so I could call upon it in the future if he was to be taken from me.

I had so few moments in my life I could characterize as real. I'd lived as Alexandra for seven years—but she wasn't me, and I wasn't her. I played a role, a role that suited Perun. They told me to be popular, so I was. They told me to be a cheerleader, so I was. They told me I loved math and hated English, so that was the way of things, even though the opposite was true. They told me not to dance, so I didn't. If I had gotten to choose, things would have been different. I sacrificed in order to serve. Serving was an honor.

For Olissa.

For my mother.

But in the moment of that kiss with Grant, with classmates milling around us, things felt real.

His questions were real.

The quickening of my heart and the buzzing in my head were real.

Real. Gloriously real. Sink-into-it-and-let-it-swallow-you real.

Unfortunately, those precious moments of realness were ripped away when a heavy hand found my shoulder. "You two should know better," said Mr. Dagby.

Grant pulled back, a redness creeping into his cheeks. "Sorry, Mr. D. See you, um, later at lunch, Lex." Grant's hand trailed off my arm, my own warmth tracking its movement. I shivered as he broke the last of our embrace, suddenly cold. He waved at me as he left then at Mr. D. "Sorry," he said again.

"I'm sorry, too," I said, turning to my locker and trying to look occupied. I touched my lips, locking in the memory of the kiss—Grant's questions, the trueness of the moment. An unexpected smile crept across my face.

A few seconds later, when my brain caught up with my heart and registered my ridiculously girly grin, I swiped it clear and told myself to get a damn grip. I could have the moment, but it couldn't have me. I had important things ahead—real-world things that needed my full attention. Being distracted by a boy wasn't an option. Perun was depending on me. I unzipped my backpack and began to transfer books. With Grant gone, I needed Dagby to find someone else to talk to so I could discreetly escape.

"Did you watch the news this morning?" asked Dagby. "Alina

Kasarian uncovered some creative accounting going on at the company she works at, C-Fusion Corp, and she turned them in. The company is a joint US/Olissan alternative…"

As Dagby trailed off, I followed his gaze to Tiff Harms and David Rinne, who were making out down the hall. Heads, hands, and arms were going every which way. Dagby's face fell into a deep scowl as he took off down the hall. His mission—to stop raging teenage hormones.

Seeing my opening, I shoved my backpack into the locker, grabbed my duffle, and headed to the back exit near the gymnasium since the front exits were monitored. I reached the back door before the first bell and cracked it open. The school backed on to a forest reserve that was just beyond a chain link fence, approximately twenty meters away. If I ran diagonally across the yard, I would only be visible to someone in the gym, but thankfully, there were no first period gym classes. I crossed my fingers for luck and bolted. I tossed the duffel over the fence as I reached it and cleared it in less than ten seconds, then scuttled behind a nearby tree.

I looked back at the school to see if any teachers were rushing out in hot pursuit of an escaped delinquent. When no one appeared, I made for the walking trail that looped through the reserve. A mile later, I left the trail, bushwhacked my way through fifteen meters of forest, and ended up on the backside of a McDonald's.

Inside the McDonald's handicapped stall, I took off the clothes marking me as an escaped high school student and replaced them with an outfit I hoped read corporate. I moved the knife from my ankle to my thigh as I exchanged jeans for a leather skirt and boots and traded my sweater for a silk blouse. I added a scarf to the ensemble, tying it in the style of an ascot, then stepped up onto the toilet and pushed the corner drop-panel to the side. One of my "go" bags was stashed in the ceiling. I had several such bags stationed around Fair Valley and the Washington DC area. They were my insurance against an unforeseen catastrophe and would help me if I needed to evade the authorities. I kept cash in each bag as well as a gun and a wig. I grabbed the gun and wig and hopped back down. I didn't normally attend my handler meetings armed, but given Varos's disappearance, I wanted to play it safe. Handler meetings always bore additional risk as they put two spies in the same place—two spies who could have been followed, two who could have been made.

The wig made me a redhead with bangs and drastically changed my appearance. With my already pale skin, it made me look Irish. Coupled with the more sophisticated clothes and a pair of wide-rimmed sunglasses, I would be unrecognizable to even Albert if he passed me on the street. I pulled my low ponytail up and secured the hair with bobby pins, then positioned the wig, using my fingers to straighten the bangs. Once everything was in place, I gave myself a thorough going over, twisting left and right in the mirror. The outfit probably added five or six years to my age, which was the whole point, really. A stray teenager out on the streets during the school period was asking for trouble.

Happy with my appearance, I put the gun in my purse along with my wallet and then put my old clothes in the duffle and zipped it. Stepping back up onto the toilet, I put the duffle next to my "go" bag and slid the drop-panel back into place.

Leaving the restroom, I joined the line of McDonald's customers, patiently and not so patiently awaiting their morning's caffeine fix. I texted Grant as I waited:

Hit w/ cramps. Gone home.

Like Albert, Grant was exceedingly embarrassed by talk of the menstrual cycle, and having received my period-related message, I knew I wouldn't hear from him for the rest of the day. Boys—such funny creatures.

With fifteen minutes to make my way to the Fair Valley Botanic Garden, I bought a newspaper and a cup of black coffee and headed out. I walked with my sunglasses on and my head bowed, sipping my coffee and pretending to skim the newspaper. I could feel my pulse quicken as I neared the garden, wondering how my life was about to change. Activated. I would have a mission. I would no longer be left to tread water and wait.

At the botanic garden, I struck out across the grassy field toward the orchid house. The day was sunny and the fall air freshly crisp. The leaves of the maples, oaks, and ash trees showed bright with oranges, reds, and yellows, and those already fallen crackled underfoot. Although cool out, sweat beaded at my brow, and I had to wipe it away. It wouldn't do to show up looking anything but calm and collected. Nerves were to be controlled. Grace in all situations was expected.

At the door of the orchid house, I took a deep breath and entered. I found it empty and took a seat opposite an assortment of purple and mauve orchids. I ran a hand along the knife at my thigh. The feel of it helped instill a sense of calm. I pulled my sunglasses off and looked at my watch. One minute to go. In sixty long seconds, someone would walk through that door, and all I'd trained for would finally begin.

7

Mistress arrived not one second early and not one second late.

"Good morning, Milena," she said, giving me a cursory smile as she took off her sunglasses.

Surprised it was her, for a second or two, I sat speechless. Although Mistress sometimes haunted my dreams, I'd never expected to lay eyes on her in the flesh again.

She surveyed me, and once I recovered myself and stood, I did the same to her. I found the years had not been kind and felt a certain pleasure in that. To hide her weight, she wore a formless black dress. She had gone completely gray, and the lines of her face, which had once seemed cunning and wise, now made her look old and tired. Only Mistress's eyes hinted at the physical strength she once had and at the power she still held.

"You look well," said Mistress.

"As do you," I replied.

She walked forward with her hand held out. I took it and kissed it lightly. I had to stoop to reach. I'd grown more than six inches since the last time we'd seen each other. It felt weird to now tower over a woman who had once loomed so large. She patted my head and then ran her fingers along my cheek. "My child, you have come a long way since that first day at Perun. My discipline did wonders for you."

Mistress gestured for us to take a seat on the bench. The bench was large, but we sat touching, thigh-to-thigh, arm-to-arm. She took my hand in both of hers and gently caressed it with her thumb. Her actions felt wrong. Like something a mother would do with a child. Unlike with my other teachers, Mistress and I had never formed a bond, and it was rare she touched me with any sort of kindness. She had hated me from our first meeting and had treated me accordingly. Although Mistress held my hand, she didn't look at me, instead facing forward. I did the same.

Her perfume was strong and cloying, and I sat there wishing orchids had more of an odor. I coughed as the smell caught in my throat. Every fiber of my being asked that I put distance between us, but I stayed rooted in place. Respect was required.

"You are my new handler?" I asked.

"I am."

"What happened to Varos? Is he okay? When I saw—"

"He is none of your concern," said Mistress, cutting me off. Hearing the sharpness of her words, I glanced in her direction and caught a look of revulsion—her eyes narrow, her mouth twisted. My stomach clenched and my heart leapt. What did that look mean? Was it merely because she still detested Varos as a human being? Or was there more behind it? At seeing my attention, Mistress recovered herself and offered a pleased smile. That smile was more disconcerting than the revolted sneer. It didn't belong on her face. The only smiles that fit Mistress were those of a sinister variety. "I am glad to see you turned out very beautiful," she offered. "Like one of these orchids. I have done well with you. How is your relationship with Gastone?"

"He loves me like a daughter," I said, turning back to the orchids. It was killing me not to have answers about Varos, but Mistress wasn't the type to give away information she deemed irrelevant to my needs. She didn't do chitchat, and my worry meant nothing to her.

Mistress nodded her approval. "I would expect nothing less. For all your faults, men have always found you appealing, even as a child."

I lowered my head to indicate I had heard but said nothing. Mistress would never let me forget my many faults. At Perun, she had constantly belittled me for not performing at a high enough standard academically, never mind I had scores surpassing most of my peers.

"Your training. You've kept up with your skills?"

Through Varos's reports, Mistress would already know the answer to this question, but as a matter of respect, I was compelled to answer her. "Yes. I faked being bullied at school so I could enroll in martial arts classes. I've studied Krav Maga, jujitsu, and judo. Albert is a gun aficionado, so I've been able to keep up my skill in that area, as well."

"You are to accompany Gastone to the gala for Kasarian?"

My stomach clenched. It was as I'd expected. I'd been called because of the gala. "Yes," I admitted.

"Excellent," said Mistress, pressing a small, hard object into my palm then closing my fingers around it. "You will use this on Kasarian's food. It must be done once the meal has begun. All food will be tested before it is served."

I opened my hand to find a vial of clear liquid. I sat there, stunned, adrenaline flooding my system, making my heart race. I broke out in an instantaneous sweat I could do nothing to hide. This wasn't supposed to happen. Of all the things I thought my activation might mean, killing was not on the list.

"Will it look like poison or something else?" I asked, hoping its effects mirrored something natural like a heart attack. If so, I might be able to continue on as Lex Gastone. If Kasarian's death was intended to look like a poisoning, however, then I knew Perun meant for me to be caught. In the age of security cameras, even the most skilled hand would likely be seen administering a poison.

"Poison," said Mistress, her voice casual, as if what she asked was no big deal.

I began to shake, my body involuntarily giving away the fact that unadulterated fear surged through me, wrapping itself around every atom of my being such that I was nothing but fear incarnate. Trying to steady myself, I locked my focus on one of the orchids in front of me, studying its every detail. Where only moments before the orchid had looked a deep, rich purple, it now appeared black. Black like the deed I was being asked to carry out. Black like the world had just become. Black like *I* would become.

I sucked in a breath. But it was all for Olissa. For my mother. I served for a purpose.

"You will be seen placing the poison, but not before it's too late for Kasarian," continued Mistress. "You are to keep your identity as Alexandra. No one must know who you really are, and we want Gastone to go down as well. Once you are in custody, say whatever you need to in order to make that happen."

I tried to hide my shock at the mention of Albert's name. In the back of my mind, I heard my instructor's words: *In war, there are always casualties, many of them innocent. We must remember the greater good.* But in all my time with Albert, I'd never dreamed he would be one of the innocents. One of the casualties.

"You will be extracted from prison in one year's time. A guard will give you a vial similar to this one. It will slow your heart rate so you appear dead. You'll be able to return home to Olissa and your family. Your service will be complete."

"I'll be done?" I blurted, not believing my ears. I'd never dreamed such a thing was possible.

"A reward for services rendered. At Perun, we take care of our people."

Home? Family? Do I even have those things back in Olissa? I'd been away so long.

"Why activate me now? That wasn't the plan."

"What do they say over here?" asked Mistress with a wicked smile. "Opportunity knocked? And no one is better than Perun at taking advantage of opportunity. We hadn't anticipated Aroyan doing so well in the campaign. And we are ahead of schedule with our en—" Mistress paused mid-sentence.

I was on the edge of my seat, wanting her to finish. Wanting all the information she was willing to impart.

Deciding she had said too much, Mistress stood to leave. Her gnarled hand took my chin, drawing my gaze up to meet hers. I felt like a small child peering up at a monster. I wanted to stand so she couldn't loom over me, but something kept me fixed in place. Mistress's grip was tight and unfriendly. "It will be hard, but you must give us the year. We are depending on you. For the blood of the fallen. For the blood of the living. For Olissa we fight."

I shuddered at hearing her words. They were the words I called upon when invading the privacy of my classmates, when seducing Grant, when lying to Albert. They were my foundation. Mistress grabbed my shoulders, digging her fingernails into my skin. "For Olissa we fight," she repeated.

"For Olissa," I said, dropping my eyes. Drawing strength from those simple words, I wrapped my fingers around the vial of poison and stood. *For my mother.*

In a year, I could go back home. I could see my family again, my blood. I could have a real life and be whomever I wanted.

I could dance.

In exchange for one year of hell, I could have freedom.

"For Olissa," I said again, this time more loudly, my voice and my purpose having grown strong.

It had begun.

8

Balmar, Olissa

I was seven. I stood at the gates of the compound, one small hand clasped by my grandmother, the other by my father. My grandmother's grip was tight, my father's tighter. They told me I'd attend a special school for gifted students, but Compound Perun looked more like a prison than a school. There was no playground or sports fields visible through the gates—only a massive gray stone building with bars over the windows. I didn't hear the laughter of any children. The only thing I heard was the sound of gunfire, and it terrified me. It was a gun's bang that haunted my dreams…that killed my mother. It had been only two weeks since her death, and the nightmares were constant. *Was it my fault she died? Was this a punishment? Didn't they love me anymore?*

My grandmother wept as the gates slowly opened, the metal hinges shrieking in protest. She grabbed me up in her arms. "Milena, I'm so sorry," she said. "Zakhar, this isn't right. My daughter wouldn't have wanted this. You promised Sibel this would never happen." I buried my face in her coat and dug my hands into the fabric, latching on with a vice grip. Something was very wrong.

"Amalya, it's Milena or one of the boys. We've no choice," said my father, his large hands encircling my waist. He pulled me from my grandmother. She shrieked. I clawed. I took part of her coat with me, the fibers of black wool embedding in my nails. "Amalya, you stay here," ordered my father. "I'll take her inside. Little O, say good-bye to your grandmother."

I began to scream and kick as my father turned me to his chest and grabbed for my legs. "Little O, please don't make a scene. This isn't a bad place. I promise."

The walk to the door of the compound seemed interminable. My father continued to talk as he walked, his voice calm. I struggled for a while, but then exhausted myself and went limp in his arms. This was the closest I'd been to my father since my mother's death. He'd withdrawn from me immediately as if I'd become tainted. I let his voice sooth me and tried to take comfort in his embrace, in the arms I'd wanted to retreat into after her death. "The Mistress will be kind to you. She's promised me that. You're important to her. She loves you." At hearing these words, I pulled myself from his chest and looked at him, hoping for further reassurances. Did I know this woman? Although his voice was soothing, his face was hard. He wouldn't look at me. "You will think her strict, but she is not without a conscience. Everything she does is for a reason." I began to struggle again, sensing the threat written in the disconnect between his face and voice. My father's embrace was not a hug but a trap, and I couldn't pretend otherwise. "She'll love you," said my father, as if saying the words would make it so.

I turned my attention back to my grandmother, willing her to save me. She stood, gripping the black iron of the gate with both hands for support. Her body shook. She looked at me with utter despair in her eyes but did nothing. Her legs buckling, she eventually sank to the ground, a crumpled swan.

"Don't fight this place, Milena. It will only make things worse for you. You must fall in line. It's the only way. This place isn't forever. Someday, you'll have another home." My father ran a gentle hand over my head. "And I hope it's a good one. I really do."

My father set me down as we reached the door, and I refused to stand. Realizing nobody was going to save me and that my fate was sealed, I stopped crying and simply sat dejected, wiping at my eyes. The door opened, revealing a sharp-featured woman with stern eyes and shiny black hair. She was dressed in a military-style uniform and stood ramrod straight.

"Stand-up, Little O. Introduce yourself," said my father, his face strangely unsympathetic—his jaw set, the furrow of his brow uncompromising. I glowered up at him but thought better of ignoring his request. I dusted myself off and straightened my clothes, all while keeping eye contact with my father. I could read nothing in his gray eyes—the color of hard steel.

I barely knew my father, having only seen him during the rare times his ship was back at port, but he had always been a loving man, not this strange creature before me. When he was home, I would dance for him, and he would clap and nod his encouragement. He called me his Little O, referring to the white swan princess, Odette, in Swan Lake. I started to hate this stranger before me. I hated him for choosing my brothers over me and for giving me away as if I was nothing. That hatred turned my fear to defiance.

"Child, you may call me Mistress," said the woman. "It is a pleasure to see you again."

I turned from my father but refused to look at Mistress. Instead, I looked at the building's gray stone. "You may call me Milena Rokva," I said. "And I do not believe we've met."

Mistress cackled at my gall. "She is a little wolf, but we shall make her a fox like me." Out of the corner of my eye, I saw her bring a hand to my father's cheek then let it fall as she looked past him to my grandmother. "I heard about your wife…"

A heartbeat passed, then another and another. The silence was long, their eyes at war. My father put a hand on my head. "I believe you will find she is her mother's daughter," he said, pulling a small, wrapped package from his pocket and offering it to Mistress.

Mistress snatched it, a hint of anger in her eyes. "Wolf, the slate is clean. You may leave. Ms. Rokva, follow me." She turned and walked away.

I glanced at my father and found him staring at Mistress with a look of surprise. "I'm sorry," he finally said before turning on his heels. I followed his progress for several seconds then spotted my grandmother. She was still on the ground. I reached a hand out— wanting to touch her warm skin and smell her scent one last time. I had wanted to be just like her, a graceful ballerina, but knew that was being taken away. She was being taken away.

"Ms. Rokva. Lesson one: you must always obey orders. Follow me," said Mistress, returning to the door. She stood so close I could feel the heat from her body.

When I refused, Mistress grabbed a fistful of cloth at my neck and hauled me backward into Compound Perun. I heard my father call to me from the gate, "Don't fight." Those were his last words to me—a command, not words of love.

As Mistress pulled, I went limp and let my shoes scrape across the floor. When Mistress finally managed to drag me around a corner and out of view, she came to stand over me. She put her boot on my chest and pushed me to the floor. The more I struggled, the more force she applied. Already exhausted by the emotions of the day, I tired quickly and eventually laid still.

"Remove your hands from my foot," said Mistress.

I did so, leaving myself completely at her mercy. Mistress moved her boot from my chest to my throat. Apparently, the promise she'd made to be kind was already forgotten. My hands reflexively went to protect myself, coming again to her foot.

"Uh, uh, uh. Hands at your sides, little wolf."

Mistress's ice blue eyes were arctic. She showed no pity for a seven-year-old child that was just abandoned. I think she reveled at the thought of breaking me. The fear I'd felt as my father carried me to the doors of Perun was now doubled. Perhaps tripled. I wet myself, the indignity of which only heightened my fear.

I held Mistress's gaze, hurling imaginary darts at her, but moved my hands off her boot. Mistress smiled at my concession. It was a grin, which grew bigger when she caught site of the puddle around my legs.

"I give you a week, my child. No one lasts more than a week."

To my credit, I lasted two before falling in line. The rules of Perun were simple.

Do what you're told.

Do not attempt to leave the compound.

Strive for excellence.

Hold Olissa above all else.

I tried running away twice during the first week. I didn't yet understand what Perun could offer me. I didn't understand that, through them, I could both honor my mother and avenge her death, along with so many others.

The first time, I never made it off the compound. I was caught trying to climb over the back rock wall. I spent the next day locked in a cell with no windows or food. Always one to learn from my mistakes, I made it outside the compound during my second attempt and to a nearby village. I was apprehended climbing into the luggage compartment of a bus bound for my hometown. I spent the next week back in the cell.

It was during that week when I first encountered Varos, the boy who later became my friend, then my handler. Varos was tasked with delivering my daily ration of water, this menial duty a punishment for his own misbehavior. During his visits, he would walk over to me and put the cup of water inside my hands, wrapping his fingers over mine for a brief moment. He could have left the cup at the door but didn't. Willing to grasp onto anything, I took comfort in this small kindness, and it helped my seven-year-old mind get through what seemed an interminable solitude. Without windows, I had no day or nights to mark the time. Early on, I spent my time planning a third escape attempt, convinced I could finally get it right. Then the solitude began to overtake me. Worry and fear started to chip away at my confidence, beating down my rebellious side. When they hauled me out of the cell, I was barely holding on to reality. The only thing keeping me from going completely insane was Varos' gentle touch each day. His simple gesture gave me hope some good might still exist in my world.

THEY CALL ME ALEXANDRA GASTONE

When I emerged from confinement, Mistress took a hot poker to my wrist. She smiled each time the poker made contact with my skin. The end result was a slightly crooked bell-shaped scar. My pain was her art.

After that week in the cell and being burned, I was reformed. Any yearnings I had for rebellion were gone. I fell in line. Hell, I jumped in line. I learned to respect my teachers, and the other cadets became my new family. I realized the good I could do if only I was properly trained.

9

"What's wrong?" asked Albert, pulling his suit jacket on and looking at my full breakfast plate with concern. "You've hardly touched your food all week. Last night, I think you had three bites. Don't think I didn't notice you giving Ork your food. And after all that work you put into making the stroganoff."

I raked the scrambled eggs with my fork, trying to make the mound look smaller. I pasted a smile onto my face for Albert's sake and forced myself to look him in the eye, something that had become increasingly hard since seeing Mistress a week prior. "I'm good. Just a little pre-dance dieting. I want to look good for the pictures. Don't worry."

Albert frowned. "You don't need to be dieting."

"Really, I'm fine. The homecoming dance is soon, and plus, I have a lot going on at school. I'm just stressed out and not very hungry."

Albert looked at his watch. "We'll talk about this more when I get home. Have fun at The University of Virginia today." He kissed my forehead.

I waved good-bye with my fork and returned to studying my plate. The thought of eating made my stomach churn. Apples, chocolate, and ginger ale were about the only things I'd been able to stomach. I was shuffling through my days like a zombie. I couldn't sleep at night. I kept seeing the old video images I'd been shown at Perun—Olissa crumbling, disappearing, American mansions, American greed. No longer a child, I now knew why I'd been shown the images, and I also knew they weren't all true. But still they haunted me. I also couldn't stop imagining what might have happened to Varos. I was hoping for the best—that he'd been made and then extracted—but already in a dark place, my mind tended to think the worst—that he'd been captured.

With no alternative, I'd become adept at compartmentalizing my feelings. Sure, there were a few bobbles now and again with Grant, but for the most part, I kept everything under lock and key. But ever since receiving my new orders, my ability to compartmentalize had inconveniently shut down, and all my relationships were suffering as a result.

I pulled the vial of poison from my pocket and set it on the counter next to my ginger ale. Kasarian's assassination on US soil was a perfect opportunity for Perun. Two enemies would be dealt with in one fell swoop—Kasarian and the United States. Albert was known to the public. He was one of the CIA's front men—a public liaison. The assassination of Kasarian by a known US scapegoat would weaken the US government in the eyes of the world, and the United States would be forced to remove their troops from Olissa or else face a backlash. The relationship between Olissa and the United States would be ruined, and Albert and I would go down in history as the cause.

To those at Perun, I would become a hero.

I grabbed the vial and stuffed it back into my pocket. The day ahead offered a break from the norm, and I hoped it would be a better distraction than school. At the very least, it would allow me to avoid Grant for a while. I had pulled further away, unable to bear his touch or his kindness. As a result, things at school were tense. Part of me wanted to throw myself into the relationship for our last few days together—go out with a bang—but that somehow seemed too selfish and cruel…crueler than the walls I was now barricading myself with. It was better I put distance between us now. It would make things easier for Grant after the gala—after I was in custody.

I was foregoing school for a senior ditch day with Martine. Our plan was a girl's day in DC full of overpriced coffee shops, desserts, and a visit to the Smithsonian for a photography exhibition called "The Unexpected." Martine was an avid photographer, so for her, it was a bit of a research trip. For me, it was simply an escape, one last hurrah with a friend. I'd already logged an excuse with Grant—a campus visit to UVA—and had done all the research I'd need in order to make both Grant and Albert believe I had visited, including knowing the bus schedule, campus tour times, and local restaurants.

* * *

Caffeinated to within an inch of my life, I found myself walking through the Smithsonian's Kogod Courtyard with Martine a few hours later. I paused to appreciate the glass canopy overhead. Outside, the day was cloudless and bright with birds flitting about. I sucked in air, trying to internalize some of that brightness.

One breath, two breaths, three breaths.

With my chest feeling painfully tight, I closed my eyes and let the sun's warmth wash over me. I desperately needed to loosen up, otherwise, I had no hope of even partially enjoying myself. I rolled my neck back and forth and then moved on to my shoulders, trying to free myself of tension.

"Come on. Hurry up," said Martine. "The exhibit is through here."

I opened my eyes with a sigh and followed dutifully after Martine. Despite the fun I was trying to have, or perhaps because of it, my mind kept turning to thoughts of what would happen after my outing at the gala. What would everyone say when the reporters showed up at their doorsteps, asking about me—the girl who poisoned Kasarian? Would Martine remember this day and say nice things?

> Reporter: "What was Lex Gastone like? Did she ever give any clue as to why she would want to kill Vladik Kasarian? What was her relationship like with her grandfather?"

Like the people who knew Ted Bundy, I imagined Martine shaking her head and looking despairingly at the camera.

> "I had no inkling she could be capable of murder."
> A pregnant pause, eyes downturned. "She was quite good at killing people in video games, though. Maybe I should have known."

My stomach flip-flopped at the thought of such an interview. Martine would recover, but I worried about Grant. He'd already been through so much in his life. Finding out you were the boyfriend to a killer would be too much to bear. He'd been good to me. My fingers brushed my lips as I remembered his kisses. Whether tender or strong, they always held such feeling behind them. He didn't deserve my betrayal.

As I followed Martine, I tried to distract myself with other, more positive thoughts, but the morbid kept invading—Albert being waterboarded, Orkney euthanized, my heroic return to Olissa and the hugs of my family while Albert rotted away in a cell. Each thought that came was darker than the last and more obscene.

Locked in my head, I again began to lag behind Martine and was startled when she grabbed my hand and pulled me forward. "Are you in sugar coma? Come on."

I shook my head to clear my thoughts and pasted on a smile. I even managed to find a laugh as an excited Martine continued to tug me forward. Rounding a corner, we found the exhibit in two large rooms. Photographs, some color and some black and white, were spaced evenly throughout. The exhibit was fairly popular with dozens of people milling about. Martine and I separated for a bit as she was drawn over, as if magnetically, to a certain photo on the far wall.

Defaulting to order, I started at the beginning and poured every ounce of my concentration into the photos in an effort to keep my thoughts at bay. The first photo was of two rather rough-looking men in orange jumpsuits, the razor wire of a prison exercise yard in the background. What made the photo interesting was not the toughness or menacing nature of the two men, but rather that they were laughing hysterically, tears streaming down their faces. Their mirth was the unexpected.

I moved to the next photo. It was of a teenage girl at a grave. Reading the accompanying sign, I learned it was her sister's grave.

Again, the tone of the photo was unexpected. The girl was happy. She had a picnic laid out before her, and the photographer had caught her talking with great animation about something joyous in her life. "That's pretty cool," I said, talking to no one in particular.

"It is," said an older woman next to me. "Very cool."

I smiled and moved to the next piece and then on down the line and around the corner. Each of the works captured an emotion but in a place you'd least expect to find it. Sadness at an amusement park, hate within a church, fear within a serene garden. By focusing on the emotions in the photographs, I was finding it easier to keep my own in check. Looking at them offered some kind of relief. It was like each photo was a pill to balance my morbid thoughts.

As a crowd moved away from a photo in the corner, I moved in, and Martine came up and tucked her arm into mine. "So what do you think? Amazing, right?"

I nodded but couldn't pull my attention from the work before me. I could see why it had drawn a crowd.

Martine nudged me. "This is one of the best ones. Makes you think, right?"

"Hmm?"

"Makes you think people are just people."

I leaned in, studying the man's eyes, looking for the lie in them.

The photo was of an Afghani warlord. He was in an armed encampment and had several weapons at his side, but his son also stood next to him. His eyes were on the boy, and his expression was full of love. He probably hated the United States and perhaps had killed many, but in that moment, he was just a father who loved his child. I could see no lie. People are just people.

I fondled the vial of poison in my pocket. The glass felt slick in my hands. "Love in an unexpected place," I mumbled, my breath catching.

"What was that?" asked Martine, squeezing my arm.

Without thinking, I pulled free of Martine, suddenly afraid to be touched.

Just one more year and then I can have it…a real life.

I turned from the photograph in a panic. *It can't be. I was careful. I couldn't have…*

I stumbled to the exhibit entrance and put a hand against the wall to brace myself, closing my eyes and trying to steady my breathing. Inside my pocket, I gripped the vial, fighting to maintain composure.

For Olissa…

The blood of the living…my grandmother and brothers.

The blood of the fallen…my mother.

10

_____

With sleep evading me, I focused on my ceiling. My glow-in-the-dark stars were in a curbside garbage bag, so except for a few chipped spots, I was looking at a blank canvas. On it, I concocted various lives for myself. Lives where I was never taken to Perun. Lives where I served Perun. Lives where I became an Olissan hero. Lives where I betrayed Perun. Lives where I ran away from it all and tried to start again.

My mind running wild with so many scenarios, I reached over and grabbed the photo of Albert and me at the Great Wall. In it, we each had an arm slung over the other's shoulders. I was smiling at the camera, and Albert was looking over at me with love in his eyes.

I'd told Mistress that Albert loved me. It wasn't an immediate thing for him, but within a year of coming to live with him, I knew it to be true. He loved me. I saw it in the smile on his face at breakfast each morning, heard it in his laughter over my conversations with Orkney, and felt it when he kissed me good-bye before school. Looking at my China photo, it was plain as day. But Mistress had failed to ask the more important question. Did I love Albert?

He wasn't just an asset. He was sweet, old Albert who wanted me to participate in his silly book club and took me on cool, educational trips every Christmas and summer. He was the man who had hung my ugly art on the fridge and who attended all my boring school events, cheering like a madman with all the other parents. He loved me. And I loved him. He was family. I'd guarded against it, but my walls had crumbled. In the house of a total stranger, while on assignment, I'd found the unexpected. I hadn't been able to say the words to Albert because I felt them and knew I shouldn't. Loving him was a failure and maybe even a betrayal.

I set Albert's photo back on my nightstand and pondered my ceiling again. One moment, I was thinking of how much I cared for Albert, and in the next, I was cursing him for teaching me to debate and question authority. Albert always asked me my thoughts on everything and had done so since the beginning. I'd been hesitant at first, but he'd slowly managed to wheedle opinions out of me. Even at our book clubs, he always made me dig deeper into the stories, including the silly romances.

"Why do you think Edward felt such an uncontrollable hunger for Virginia's…uh, company?"

"Because he's horny?"

"And?"

"And one evolutionary avenue for men is to spread their seed far and wide to ensure their genes make it into the next generation."

A nod of approval from Albert, then another question. *Why do you think Virginia gave up her virtue so easily?*

Because she's horny, and he's hot?

"And?"

"And she was a free-thinking woman unwilling to be confined in her actions by the morals of conventional society."

During our trips, we were never just tourists snapping pictures and saying "oh, that's interesting" or "oh, that's pretty." We read history books about each place before visiting. We talked about how and why each culture differed from ours. We didn't judge. We only observed and learned.

Was the United States' presence in Olissa really a bad thing? They'd helped to rebuild after the last invasion. Health care had improved. There were more schools. Higher literacy rates. Less crime. As far as occupiers go, the Americans seemed pretty benign, but what if they had helped to rig the election, insuring Kasarian's victory? And what of the reports about US companies acting fraudulently? Even Alina Kasarian, who was as pro-United States as her brother, had uncovered wrongdoing.

Still, of all Olissa's enemies, surely the United States was the least malicious and had done the least damage. They weren't killing or imposing rules that stripped Olissans of their cultural rights and heritage. They were just a bodyguard of sorts. It wasn't the US government's fault American companies were behaving badly. Companies behaved badly all the time, all over the world.

Staring at my ceiling, I could feel tears of frustration threatening to escape. It was a foreign sensation. I couldn't remember the last time I'd cried. As I gave in, tears burst forth, slathering my cheeks. I rolled over and sunk my head into a pillow, in part to stifle my sobs but also to smother the feelings I had no use for.

Why was I thinking so much? Why was I questioning Perun now, after all these years? I'd been given orders. My feelings for Albert didn't matter. In just a year, I could be back in Olissa. I could return to my grandmother and brothers and have a real life. Maybe even dance again.

For the blood of the fallen. For the blood of the living. For Olissa we fight.

There was such a beautiful sentiment in the words I'd spoken at the beginning and end of each day at Perun—I was fighting for the blood of my ancestors, who endured countless years of war, sometimes whole lifetimes of it. I was fighting for my mother, who had died. I could still remember her blood on my hands—a sleek, angry red—as if her death had happened yesterday. I could still feel my heart stall as life faded from her broken body. I was fighting for the living—my grandmother, my brothers, my friends. People who deserved to live without fear. I was fighting for a nation that had clawed itself back into existence again and again. A nation whose spirit couldn't die.

But I could feel my resolve cracking and wondered why I faltered. In my seven years with Albert, I'd never once thought of betraying Perun. Albert had treated me well, and I had everything a girl could want, but I'd still never considered it. Was I afraid of jail? Torture?

Staring at the ceiling, I pondered these questions, demanding honesty from myself. Was I afraid?

Searching, I found the answer was both yes and no. Yes, I was afraid. Who wouldn't be? But no, I wasn't too afraid to act. It was only a year. I could endure a year. Fear wasn't breaking me. It was love.

Albert was so like my mother, such a gentle soul. They had similar smiles, always with a tinge of humor lurking in the background like they were somehow wiser than everyone else in the room. In a different time and place, they would have liked each other.

I wiped my eyes and sat up, digging the vial of poison out from under my pillow. I set it in my lap along with Albert's photo and thought back to all my friends at Perun, the people who became my family. I could still see their faces so vividly; remember what they loved, what they hated, what they feared. There was Varos, the boy whose kind heart got me through solitary, and Isra, the leader of the girls—my closest friend next to Varos. I'd pitied Zhanna and Luka, the doomed lovebirds, destined to be forever separated once they left Compound Perun. I'd left behind a vast community at Perun—Aysel, Elene, Rolan, Rem, Abel, Sencer—some were friends for only months, some for years, but I was shaped by each and every one of them.

For most of us, the years at Perun were hard but rewarding. The training left us battered, but we were working for a cause. We had teachers to guide us and friendships to support us. I could have been truly happy at Perun if not for Mistress. She had a special brand of hate for me. Some days she was civil, even encouraging, but on others, especially when she'd been drinking, I could not escape her wrath. On more than one occasion, she pulled me from bed in the middle of the night. *You're a 'Necessary.' I never wanted you*, she'd hiss over and over, throwing me to the floor. "Your father was an idiot. A damn idiot." Like my first day at the compound, her boot would come to my throat as she glared down at me, rage in her eyes.

The commotion always drew the other cadets, and the older ones would step forward to soothe Mistress and talk her down, somehow reasoning with her through her drunken haze. Eventually, a teacher would lead Mistress off to her quarters while my friends picked me up off the floor. Without question or comment, Isra would take me back to bed and curl up beside me. To distract me from what had happened, she'd gently caress my hair while whispering a story. Fantastical tales of warrior princesses battling evil in far off lands were her favorite. With Isra watching over me, I could somehow find sleep again. Without her, I would have faced many sleepless nights at Perun. The cadets were my mentors, friends, and heroes. Before I left Compound Perun, each of the cadets hugged me as a friend and then shook my hand as a fellow soldier-in-arms. Although many of us would not see each other again, we believed ourselves to be forever bonded by a common mission.

And now, by questioning my mission, I was spitting in their faces.

I folded into a fetal position and reached within myself for Perun, for the hands of my fellow cadets. I reached into my depths, but Perun was already too far gone. Perun had fallen away while I was distracted. By threatening Albert, their hold on me was broken. I sobbed, wanting my clarity of purpose back. I wanted things to be simple again. I wanted to know who I was supposed to be. I was giving up a chance at a real life, all to protect a man in a false reality. Part of me thought I was crazy, but the other part knew it had to be this way. The world had already stolen my mother; they couldn't have Albert, too.

I felt naked and bare without Perun's cloak. In its place, I only had Albert, and despite having chosen him, I wasn't sure he could fill the void. By abandoning Perun, I was abandoning Olissa, my homeland. Her history, pride, and perseverance were part of my ancestry, and I was leaving her to fend for herself. I was abandoning my grandmother and brothers and my future. I wished Perun's original plan for me hadn't changed. I would have happily passed them CIA secrets when asked. Or if they had only wanted Kasarian dead from a heart attack, I could have done that, as well. I didn't like the idea of killing, but I could have done it. I would have done it for Olissa.

But my time to wallow was over. I'd made my choice, and now I needed to follow through. I shoved my bare feet into a pair of old tennis shoes and tiptoed out of my bedroom with the vial in hand.

I exited the house and walked to the curb. I felt heavy as I walked, but also strong. I was choosing love, choosing Albert.

I opened the trash bin, untied the top bag, and dropped the vial inside.

Now I needed a new plan. I couldn't betray Perun and expect to walk away. Betrayal meant cancellation. Once they realized my disloyalty, I'd be killed within days. By loving Albert, I was going to have to leave him.

11

Listening to Ork snore, I watched the minutes slowly move forward on my alarm clock…1:43…44…45…46. I sighed and turned to the blank canvas of my ceiling. My mind kept turning to the future as I concocted new lives for myself. New names: Diana, Kara, Mia. New jobs: waitress, clerk, cook. I began the story of many new lives, but finished none of them. It wasn't fun to think of a new future. I was leaving too much behind. I told myself I could finally be "me," but somehow that didn't make it any better. It didn't make any of my possible futures brighter. Without the people in Alexandra or Milena's life, the color palette of what lay before me seemed dull. Muted.

Lost in thoughts leading me farther and farther from sleep, I was startled when my phone chimed with a text. Relieved at the possibility of a momentary distraction, I snatched it off my nightstand.

R u awake?

The text was from Grant. I stared at it hungrily, like it was a cure for my insomnia—the pill, the panacea. His voice. If I could only hear his voice, one of his silly bedtime stories. My finger flew to the 1 button to speed dial him, but then I caught myself. I was going to have to run. I had no choice. Things for Grant and I hadn't changed. I rolled back over, cradling the phone to my chest.

With a finger hovering over the 1, my mind bombarded me with admonishments. *Don't lead him on. Don't be so weak. He doesn't deserve the wake of what I'm leaving behind. He doesn't deserve it. Damn it, he doesn't deserve it.*

I slammed my eyes shut, willing myself to have strength. I thought of a new name, a new job—Lana, the barista by day and student by night. Grant's voice kept intruding on my story...*Penn is only an hour away from Princeton.*

My eyes brimming with tears, I hit speed dial. I was weak, weak, weak. Pathetic.

"Hello?" said a surprised Grant.

"Can't sleep?" I asked.

"Nope. Been trying for hours. I can't stop thinking. I didn't wake you, did I?"

"I was awake."

Grant didn't reply. A silence hung in the air. I didn't know what to say. In Grant's voice, I could hear he wanted to talk...to talk about us. To talk about my behavior—the terrible push and pull I was subjecting him to. But I couldn't talk about that stuff. It was a moot point. I was leaving. Yet, I wanted to hear more of his voice. I wanted him to talk and to keep on talking.

"I want—" said Grant, finally breaking the silence.

"Can you tell me a story?" I replied, quickly interrupting.

Grant sighed, with annoyance or relief, I couldn't tell. "Sure. I can do that. Hmmm...let me think... Okay, I've got one... Space, the final frontier. The starship Enterprise is on a five-year mission to explore strange—"

"Grant?"

"Lex? What is it?"

"Can you tell me that one from a couple of months ago? The one set in California?"

Grant laughed quietly. "The one about a future us?"

"Yep, that one. That's the one I want to hear," I said, nodding my head and tucking my comforter up under my chin.

"The year is 2025. You're sitting at a café table overlooking the beach. I haven't seen you in years. We broke up during our first year of college. You'd met some guy named Ezekial, a philosopher, and dumped my ass. But there you are as I pass by, an apparition from my past.

"I'm in California on business for my law firm. One of the firm partners was supposed to make the trip but got sick, and I was sent instead. Looking at you, I think maybe it was destiny that brought me back to you. Fate.

"The air smells of equal parts salt water and coffee…"

"Thank you," I mumbled, letting his voice carry me. Soothe me. I could feel the sweep of relaxation beginning at my heart and radiating outward.

"I'm nervous as I walk up to you. It's been so long, but you look the same. Those same beautiful eyes. At feeling me near, you look up. You smile that crooked smile. The smile only you have. The smile I always loved…"

Grant continued to talk, but I couldn't hear him.

My eyes flicked open.

My muscles tensed.

Notions of sleep leapt away.

THEY CALL ME ALEXANDRA GASTONE

He changed the story.
The smile. He added the damn smile.
Alexandra's crooked smile.
Not mine.

12

I left early the next morning, before Albert had even gotten out of the shower, and went to a cyber café in town instead of school. I was paranoid about having my internet activity monitored by Perun and figured a cyber café was safer than even the computers at school. Having chosen to betray Perun, I was less than a week away from an assassin's bull's-eye. I had my "go" bags, but those were designed to help me evade US authorities until I could contact Perun. Now I needed to evade Perun and disappear for good. There was only one person I knew who could help me do that, and he was off the radar.

Although I'd hoped to be lulled to sleep by Grant's story, his added embellishments had the opposite effect, which proved to be surprisingly lucky. After getting off the phone with him, I started to think about the one person who knew the real me—Varos. We'd known each other for almost eleven years, and he knew me as both Milena and Lex.

I'd started to think about Varos and our interactions before his disappearance. The norm was for us to meet for fifteen to thirty minutes each month so he could assess my mental state and focus. Although once a friend, the meetings were businesslike. Quick and efficient. That is until recently, when the sessions had grown less formal. He'd suddenly wanted to know about my happiness. He'd asked about Orkney and whether I had any friends that were just for me and not Perun. He'd asked if I liked to hike and said he'd been reading blogs by people who had hiked the Appalachian Trail and been transformed. I'd been evasive in answering his questions, worried he was somehow testing me. However, thinking back on it and on Mistress's face when I'd asked about Varos, a different reason for his questions dawned on me. His disheveled appearance and baggy clothes, which I'd taken as Varos being too busy to care, on further consideration, seemed like a possible means of hiding weight loss, the beard a way to hide the changing character of his face.

Perhaps the biggest change, and what probably should have been an immediate heads-up, was the almost-kiss. We were sitting on a park bench, and he'd turned to me, his eyes searching.

"Lex…Little O…at Perun… I know this is going to sound strange and out of the blue…but did you have a crush on me?"

I went wide-eyed, my face turning an embarrassed crimson. Although Varos was older than me, I'd had a crush on him from my early days at Perun. I didn't see the extra pudge or the physical weakness—all I saw was his brightness and wit. I marveled at his mind, wishing I might someday match him. I'd never acted on the crush and had told no one. Seven years is a big gap when you're a kid. I knew he wouldn't be interested.

Dumbfounded, I sat mute. I didn't understand how he could have known. Or why he was bringing it up. Was this some sort of test? Was he about to tell me some anecdotal story about keeping my emotions in check like I'd done with him? But why the Little O? After learning of my father's nickname and the meaning behind it, Varos had latched onto it while we were at Perun. But he'd never used it on the outside. Never.

Varos leaned closer. He brought a hand to my face, tucking a stray hair behind my ear. For a second or two, our eyes found each other. He leaned closer again, only inches away. I was so confused. What was happening? Varos had touched me hundreds of times over the years, but now his hand on my skin burned, a pleasant fire of sensation. I peered into Varos's eyes, searching for an answer. His motive? Taught by Perun to be wary of people's motivations, all I could think was it was a test. But my senses hummed. Hummed like they sometimes did with Grant when I let my guard down.

Grant's face flashed before me as Varos's lips brushed mine for the most infinitesimal of moments. I jerked away and leapt to my feet. I still hadn't said a word. I was incapable. I walked to a nearby tree and stood against it, looking away. I focused on the leaves of an oak, watching them dance and sway, their fall colors just beginning to appear. I took ten breaths and then turned around.

I found Varos gone. No good-bye. No nothing.

Because of the changes in Varos and that almost-kiss, I thought there was a chance, albeit a small one, he hadn't been made or captured but was on the run. The tail I had was Perun assessing my loyalty after Varos's betrayal. Judging from his questions to me, I also thought he might want a partner. I knew the odds were high I was concocting an elaborate delusion to give myself some hope, but I had to try to reach Varos on the off chance I was right.

At the cyber café, I found an open computer in the back and connected. My hands paused over the keyboard as I thought back to Perun and Varos. Perun was established after the last period of occupation in Olissa. The Soviet Union, Iran, Turkey—they had all controlled Olissa at one point or another, and the founders of Perun recognized independence would never be assured near such giants as long as Olissa held so little power.

The majority of cadets were brought up from birth hearing the dogma surrounding the Olissan independence movement and knowing they would be brought to Perun one day. They and their parents were part of a movement. Despite my father's words as we walked to the doors of Perun, words indicating he was somehow entangled with Perun, I hadn't been raised in the movement. My family lived in the countryside. We went to Murdan, a nearby town, for groceries and the dance academy and that was it. Our lives were relatively untouched by politics. Olissa had been independent since I was born. Peace was all I knew. It was all I knew until the day my mother died.

The other children at Perun sensed I didn't belong, that I didn't understand what the stakes were. For reasons I didn't understand at the time, Mistress called me a "Necessary," and the other cadets initially latched onto that terminology. They acted like I was some sort of necessary evil they had to endure. I was the poor scholarship kid attending an elite prep school. Varos, seven years my senior, was the first to accept me, helping to thaw my social status.

A genius with tech but also physically weak, Varos could have been easily shunned by the other cadets were it not for his innate charm and quick wit. At Perun, where our lives were regimented and our training brutally rigorous, Varos's ability to amuse and make us laugh during our downtime made him one of the most liked of the cadets.

I remembered the arrival of one new cadet named Tamaz who thought he might ingratiate himself with the other cadets by picking on the weakest. He targeted Varos and tried to embarrass him by stealing his clothes while he was in the shower and then calling us all out to watch. Much to Tamaz's surprise, Varos emerged from the bathroom proudly wrapped in a toilet paper toga, a big grin on his face. He danced down the hall to the cheers of the other cadets and then stopped to bow in front of Tamaz. "Stealing the fat kid's clothes? Really, that's the best you could come up with?" Varos shook his head, disappointed in Tamaz's efforts. "You don't have the smarts to best me." He held out his hand. "I suggest you be my friend instead."

Varos had a treacherous tongue and an uncanny ability to sense a person's emotional weaknesses. Tamaz, for example, wasn't particularly intelligent and was acutely sensitive about it. Without breaking a sweat or taking a punch, Varos had silenced him.

Although Varos had been kind while I was in confinement, he truly befriended me after one of my daily scraps with a bully named Okan. Okan was tall for his age and burly. He had wide-set eyes that never grew larger than slits and a nose with crooked nostrils he liked to flare. At Perun, those recruits intended for operational roles received a special diet. We were allotted a portion of food, which supplied us with the perfect balance of vitamins and nutrients for our height and weight. Okan believed they'd made a miscalculation in determining his food ration and liked to steal my food to supplement his own meager portions. Varos had been the one to pick me up off the floor at the end of a rather quick fight in morning mess. He set me on my feet then whispered in my ear,

"Go for the nuts next time. The jewels are always a man's weakness."
When I looked at him with confusion, Varos's face crinkled into a
smile. He grabbed his crotch. "The jewels."

I didn't wait to try out my new strategy. When Okan went to
deposit my breakfast tray at the mess counter, I tapped him on the
back. He turned. Finding me, he leered. I smiled back and kicked
him in the crotch with all the force I could muster. Much to the
amusement of both myself and the other cadets, Okan spent the
next several minutes on the ground curled up in the fetal position,
his face beet red and sweat pouring off his brow. Okan never
bothered me again, and I got my first taste of comradery with the
other cadets as several gave me an appreciative pat on the back.

After all he'd done for me, it was no wonder I developed a
crush. Varos and I talked about everything, including what we
hoped to accomplish for Olissa and our fears of failing Perun. Given
his devotion to Olissan independence, I could barely believe he had
run, despite evidence to the contrary.

With a cursor blinking asking for a command, I pulled my
focus back into the present. With no way of contacting Varos via
phone—he always used a burner and then discarded it—I was left
with no assured way of getting in touch, only faint possibilities. I
knew he had been visiting hiking blogs about the Appalachian Trail,
so I went to WordPress and constructed just such a blog using the
name Odette Fox, a moniker based on my two nicknames at Perun.
Varos called me Little O, while to Mistress I was the silver fox. In
my opening blog post, I weaved keywords and phrases like "change
of circumstance," "bull's-eye," "evasion," and "travel companion
desired" into the entry. Once I was finished with my own blog,

I started pulling up other A.T. blogs and leaving messages in the comments section using the same name and keywords.

Having submitted the last of my comments, I remained seated, the full weight of what I had done finally overwhelming me. My life as I knew it was coming to an end. My only option was to run, which meant hurting Albert, Grant, Martine and all of the people who called me a friend. I hated to think of Albert believing I had run away, or worse, been kidnapped and killed. Could I somehow fake my death?

I thought back to Perun and my failed escape attempts and wondered if running was even a viable option. If I had to run without Varos, how many months would I have before they found me? Even with Varos at my side, there was a good chance we'd be caught eventually—whether months or years, they *would* find us. I rubbed a finger along the smooth scar at my wrist. If I ran, Mistress would seek vengeance. A quick bullet to the brain would be a kindness I wouldn't deserve. I envisaged something like what happened before the switch with Alexandra in Prague, only prolonged over a period of weeks.

A text from Albert interrupted my musings.

> *FYI dinner's covered tonight. Take out. See you at 6.*
> *Have something to discuss.*

* * *

I couldn't help but fidget as I waited for Albert to come home. I was guessing he either wanted to talk about my eating habits or the fact I'd missed both first and second period while at the cyber café. Whatever Albert wanted to discuss, I didn't want to waste any of our remaining time together talking about something that wasn't even an issue. I wanted to play chess and talk about more books. I only had a couple of days before I'd have to leave with or without help from Varos, and I wanted to spend them doing all the things Albert loved.

I purposefully put out some M&Ms and popcorn on the coffee table to try to assuage any potential eating disorder fears Albert might have. I even ate some of the M&Ms and popcorn, although Ork got a lot of the latter. Needing a distraction, I pondered working on the research report for Dagby—it was due the next day—but then decided on torturing myself in a different way. Why bother with homework when I was about to become a dropout? A couple months back, when I'd hosted the cheer squad bonding night, one of the girls had left behind a celebrity magazine. In it, I'd stumbled upon a friend from my past—Isra, whose kind touch and wild stories were the healing balm that helped to collect and soothe me after one of Mistress's unprovoked attacks. From the magazine, I learned Isra now bore the name Anna Kincaid and Anna was a New York socialite, scheduled to marry Michael Wilcox, Jr., a US senator, by the month's end. Next to Varos, Isra was my closest friend. Although only a few years older, Isra had a natural maternal instinct and fell into a leadership role with the female cadets. Queen Bee, she watched out for us, and we tried to make her proud.

Isra was tall and willowy. She had flowing blond hair, vibrant green eyes, and was one of the prettiest girls I had ever seen. At Perun, I wasn't the only one with a nickname bestowed by Mistress. Okan, the boy who initially bullied me until I put him down with a kick to the nuts, was the bear—a fighter. Varos was the crow—

smart but a nuisance. And Isra was the dove—the beauty.

According to Mistress, all animals had a purpose in nature as each cadet had a purpose within Perun. My purpose as a fox was to be cunning. Given her distaste for me, I'm unsure why Mistress was so keen for my transformation into a fox like herself, but whatever her motivations, she worked hard to rid me of my more quarrelsome, wolf-like qualities. Judging from the magazine spread, Isra's purpose was to be pretty and marry someone of strategic importance. At learning of her cover identity, I thought it was sad she'd been tasked with only a valentine role. Mistress underestimated Isra by calling her the dove. Isra was beautiful but not fragile like a dove. Not in the least. She was the glue holding us together.

I reclined on the couch with my magazine to look at my old friend and ponder how life was for her. How was she handling living a lie? Was it a thrill? A burden? Something in between? I looked at Michael's photo. He carried himself like a powerful man, but there was also a kindness to his face. In one photo, he had an arm protectively around Anna's waist as he led her through a crowd. How did Isra feel about her future husband? Did he mean nothing to her? I couldn't imagine her being that cold, but perhaps I was wrong. Maybe I was the one underestimating Isra's abilities. I ran a finger over her beautiful face, remembering her quiet strength. What would she think of me if she learned of my betrayal?

As I sat lost in thought, my hand absently came to my neck, searching for the locket I wore. Alexandra's habit of sliding it back and forth along its chain had become my habit. I fumbled with the collar of my shirt as my hand came up empty and then looked to my lap to see if it had fallen. There was nothing.

I sat up, struggling against a wave of panic. I began diving my hands between the couch cushions. The locket anchored me to Alexandra. I couldn't lose it. I needed it. I needed it in order to be her.

Finding only crumbs between the cushions, I fell to my knees to look under the couch.

Dust bunnies.

The locket was gone.

13

"Chow time Lex…" called Albert, clomping in from the garage. "I picked up pasticcio from the Greek restaurant near work. So no diet tonight."

"Yum!" I called from the kitchen, trying to sound enthusiastic despite my private nausea. I'd scoured every inch of the downstairs and the truck and hadn't found the locket. All I wanted to do was go upstairs to continue the search. "I've already got the table set," I hollered, trying to settle my emotions. I didn't have much time left with Albert and I wanted to make the most of it.

Albert bustled toward the table, Ork having magically appeared on his heels. "How was your day, Orkney?" asked Albert.

I smiled at seeing the pair, and my heart tightened. They were my two old men. My gentle giants. I took a mental snapshot of the pair so I could call upon it later once I'd left.

I grabbed some sodas and met Albert and Ork at the table. Ork was already nose-down in a takeout box of moussaka.

At seeing Albert's gift for Ork, a lump rose in my throat. "You're awesome, you know that?" I said to Albert.

"Sure do," said Albert, handing me a box of food and taking a seat. His eyes twinkled mischievously.

"So you wanted to discuss something?" I asked, wanting to get the mystery over with.

"Yes, yes. Do you want the good news or the bad news?" asked Albert.

"Good," I said, my curiosity piqued.

Albert grinned ear-to-ear. "I got a call today."

"Yeah?"

"It was from my friend at Princeton. You got in! You'll get the formal offer of admission in a week or two. Lex, I'm so proud of you," said Albert, reaching across to pat my hand. "You're going to make a wonderful addition to the school, and I know you'll love it there as much as I did."

I threw a hasty smile onto my face and somehow found some enthusiasm for a response. "That's awesome, Grandpa. I can't believe it." My stomach was knotted. I should have started with Albert's bad news. With only a few days left of being Alexandra, good news about the life I could have had felt like being kicked in the gut. I would never go to Princeton. I wasn't even going to finish high school.

"Princeton's playing football against Harvard in a couple weeks. The Ivy matchups are always fun, and I was thinking we might do a little road trip and catch the game? I know you probably don't think it's super cool to hang out with your grandpa, but I can treat you to some Princeton sweatshirts and show you the best place to grab pizza. What do you say?"

I could feel my face burn as I fought back tears. It hurt to see Albert so excited. He was going to be devastated when I simply vanished. "Of course I'll go to the game with you. And Grandpa, you know I love hanging out with you. You don't need to bribe me.

I'm going to miss you so much when I'm gone. I lo—"

"Good, I was hoping you'd say that," said Albert, reaching into the front pocket of his blazer. "Because that brings me to my second bit of good news." Albert reached across the table and handed me an envelope. "I know you've wanted this for a long time, and I've been putting you off, but with the news about Princeton, I thought it was time you got your way."

Without even opening the envelope, my heart caught. I knew what was inside. Since coming to live with Albert, we'd taken two trips a year, one over Christmas break and the other during summer. Although Albert was democratic about book club night, he hadn't been regarding our trip destinations. He always asked for my opinion, but then chose to ignore it in favor of trips that were educational and thought provoking. For the last three years, I'd been begging for an adventure vacation in New Zealand, full of hiking, white water rafting, horse trekking, and bungee jumping. I'd campaigned hard, but Albert had always put me off. Given his age, I never really blamed him.

Despite my best efforts, a few stray tears escaped. "You didn't," I said, opening the envelope.

Albert laughed. "I most certainly did. We're going this Christmas. Two weeks in Godzone. That's what the Kiwi's call New Zealand. It'll be summer so the weather is going to be great, and we'll do all those activities you've wanted to do, although I'm absolutely not bungee jumping. You can do it, but don't try to pressure me into it with one of your bribes or bets."

I laughed, wiping away a few more tears.

"I hope those are tears of joy and excitement," said Albert.

I smiled and nodded. Although I had to leave him, I knew I'd made the right decision in choosing to save Albert. I was lucky to have as many years with him as I did. "You need to bring me down off the high I'm on. What was your bad news?" I asked, grabbing my can of ginger ale.

Having just deposited a forkful of food into his mouth, Albert held up a finger as he quickly chewed and then swallowed. He wiped a napkin across his mouth as he cleared his throat. Albert's expression was pained. "I'm afraid I have to rescind my invitation to the gala. I know you were excited to go, but I learned today the threat level surrounding Kasarian's visit was increased. There's chatter a group called Perun will strike. All plus-ones for lower-tiered guests have been elim—"

I choked on my ginger ale at Albert's mention of Perun and had to pound my chest to clear it. My mind immediately swam with questions. How did Albert know of Perun? Made up of sleeper agents, Perun's public profile was almost non-existent. There shouldn't have been any chatter unless… I stared at Albert dumbfounded, my thoughts spinning out of control. Was I wrong about Varos? Had he actually been caught? Had he caved under torture and given me up? Did the man sitting across from me know who I was? Was he testing me?

"Oh," I said, not really knowing how to respond. Although I kept my face impassive, my muscles coiled, ready for flight. I had a "go" box buried near the dog park. If I ran at top speed, I could grab it and be gone in less than ten minutes.

Albert patted my hand again. "I'm sorry."

I trembled at his touch and slid my hand away, hiding it in my lap. Needing to run from Perun, I'd been in an impossible situation, and Albert had just handed me an out. His news about the gala was good, if true. But that kind of luck didn't just happen in the spy world.

"Per-en?" I asked, purposefully stumbling over the pronunciation. "Never heard of them."

Albert nodded solemnly, "Pear-une. A group of radical Olissan rebels. They've been silent for years, but with Aroyan narrowly losing the election… Well, I guess they see an opening."

"Hmmm," I said, shaking my head in understanding. Albert looked calm and collected and not at all like someone who was about to jump across the table and slap on some handcuffs. "Well, that's disappointing about the gala, but I understand."

I smiled at Albert hesitantly. Had I really just won the spy world's version of the lotto? Was I really that lucky? Could I allow myself to get excited about Princeton? About New Zealand? My heart quickened at the thought of keeping my life as Alexandra. And what if Grant got into Penn? He'd only be an hour away.

I picked up the tickets to New Zealand and tapped them on the table. Surely, Albert wouldn't have shown them to me if he knew. Or told me about Princeton. I knew Albert. He wouldn't bait me—he wasn't that cruel.

I smiled again, this time with measured excitement. "You know how you could make the gala up to me," I said, grabbing my fork, a sense of relieved giddiness taking hold.

Albert eyed me. "And how would that be?"

I held my fork high in the air and then swooped it down to my plate. "You could go skydiving with me in New Zealand," I said with a laugh.

Albert rolled his eyes. "I love you, but I'm not doing that either. Not in a million years."

I studied Albert for a moment; studied his look of loving yet annoyed affection. My giddiness dissipated, replaced by feelings of warmth and peace. I reached across and put a hand on Albert's arm, "I love you, too, Grandpa."

14

I went upstairs after dinner and began a full-on search for the missing locket. I thought I remembered having it on when I'd left for the cyber café, but maybe not. I took the locket off to shower, so I checked my bathroom first. Coming up empty, I then checked my bedside tables, under the bed, under Ork's bed, in all my drawers, under the bedspread, and in the trash. Nothing. Nothing. Nothing.

When I was moved to Prague before my insertion, I spent my days watching surveillance videos of Alexandra as I recuperated from plastic surgery. I watched them incessantly, studying this girl I was being asked to become. In the videos, Alexandra touched the locket often. Sitting outside and reading, she would slide it back and forth along the chain. Talking with her parents or friends, she'd reach up and absently run a finger over the gold surface.

After seven years, I still remembered the locket being taken from Alexandra and placed around my neck. I was unable to walk, so Raykom held me in his arms while Negar pulled Alexandra's crumpled body from the crash. The car burned, and smoke was heavy in the air. Raykom waved his free arm wildly, trying to keep the smoke away from us, but it still singed my throat and nostrils.

Visible through the hazy veil, I could see Alexandra wasn't yet dead. Even with my excruciating injuries, she fascinated me, and we blinked at each other with nearly identical eyes. Where only minutes before I'd seen her through the car window, singing and laughing, this was a new Alexandra. One in tragedy, in pain. She mouthed the word "help," but I could do nothing. Couldn't she see I was her enemy? Couldn't she see they had broken me, too? I watched as Negar reached for the clasp of her necklace. Alexandra brought a hand up to stop him, but it was batted away. The same gruff hands that stripped the locket placed it around my neck. The chain dug into my skin as he fumbled the clasp over and over until finally latching it.

I wore the locket to remind myself of that night and that broken little girl. I wore it to remind myself she had lived and had suffered for the cause. Now, due to my own lack of care, it was gone. It was the one thing tying me to the real Alexandra Gastone. She had touched it. Loved it. Cared for it.

The cyber café and school were the only places left to look, so I finally gave up the search and plopped down onto my bed with my backpack, pushing thoughts of the locket to the side. With a new lease on Alexandra's life, I was behind in my homework. Dagby's paper was due the next day, and I couldn't afford to keep worrying about the locket, no matter how much it meant to me. I didn't want Princeton rescinding their offer because of a plummeting history grade. Perun would no doubt want a return to their old plan for me, which meant college and then the CIA. I told myself the locket had to be at school. I was good at finding things, and the locket would be no different.

I looked at my phone and thought about calling Grant now that I was staying put, but then decided against it. I'd start fresh with

Grant the next morning. I'd be a better girlfriend. I'd somehow find a way to be "close but far" without Grant knowing I was keeping my emotions in check. I could make him happy. I just needed to figure out how.

I pulled out all the research materials I had for Dagby's report on political secrets and spread them out in a wide U-shape, then opened my computer and found my file for the report. A mostly blank page with only a title taunted me: *The Secret of Tarkan Aroyan and How Things Might Have Been Different.* I groaned. Even the title needed more work. "The answer is written plain as day, in black and white," I said out loud, recalling Albert's hint. I scanned the mess of research papers looking for something to pop out as obvious, and then rolled my eyes when no great revelations presented themselves. "Jeez Albert, thanks for that bit of insight."

Ork barked from his doggie bed.

"What do you think?" I asked. "Should I start researching FDR, or should I keep at it?"

Ork barked five times in quick succession and then thumped his tail as if daring me to quit.

I grabbed a dog biscuit out of my drawer and tossed it to Ork, who caught it midair like a pro. "Thanks for the pep talk, babe. You're right. Nobody likes a quitter."

I opened a couple of the research books I had—biographies that had been rushed to press when the Olissan presidential campaign became interesting—and peered down at their pages. I'd received extensive eidetic memory training at Perun where they taught me how to access and recall information by storing it systematically, using easily remembered imagery and associations. Because of my training, I knew the content of each page, but maybe because I was rusty, having the pages in view helped to order my thoughts.

I began to flick through the books, reviewing Aroyan and Kasarian's early histories. Although the secret was Aroyan's, I was researching both men as they'd known each other for over twenty years, having served together in the Olissan military. I wanted to cover all my bases, as the secret might have to do with their relationship. Early on, they had been friends.

The two men could not have led more different lives. Tarkan Aroyan was raised by a sometimes-single mother who was a law secretary by day and a husband hunter by night—she wasn't much of a mother or wife by all accounts. She married six times. While Tarkan attended local schools and worked a job to help out, Vladik Kasarian and his much younger sister, Alina, led privileged lives, their father, Pavle, a descendent of the Olissan royal family. Although the Kasarians hadn't held power in over two hundred years, Pavle was still one of the richest and most well-known men in Olissa. After being dethroned, the family moved into philanthropic work and was heavily involved in post-war rebuild projects.

Except for nearly dying from a nut allergy at the age of five and then again at fifteen, Vlad's life had been relatively charmed until his parents were killed in a helicopter crash, and Alina's back was broken. It was an accident he narrowly missed being a part of, arriving at the helipad only minutes after their departure. Political pundits believed it was Kasarian's royal ancestry coupled with the presence of his scarred and handicapped sister that made him popular with the Olissan public—of royal blood, he embodied Olissa's past but was also seen as one of the people. He suffered as they did.

I studied a photograph of Vlad and Tarkan from their military days. They were all of twenty years old, young and fresh-faced with a casual arm slung over each other's shoulders. Looking at the photo, I wondered if either man could have fathomed the shift that would occur in their relationship? How ugly it would become?

I began to turn something over in my mind. "The answer is plain as day, in black and white." I looked to Ork. "Albert said something else as well. He said it was out there for everyone to see." Pulling my computer into my lap, I smiled. "That's the real clue. I need to look in the mainstream media where everyone would see it. I've bogged myself down in the details. I need a wider angle."

My fingers tingled with excitement as I brought up the Edunews site and clicked on the first of their videos on the presidential campaign. I'd seen the videos before but now watched with new eyes. I examined each one four times, trying to take everything in. Trying to look for what was most obvious. By the end, I was so frustrated I wanted to scream. Even with my spy training, I couldn't discern anything important from the videos, obvious or otherwise.

At hearing my stomach growl, I figured a quick snack break was in order. Maybe after a breather, I would have fresher eyes. In the kitchen, I couldn't decide between sweet or salty, so I grabbed a package of chocolate chip cookies and a bag of potato chips and plopped down at the breakfast bar. It felt so good to be hungry again. For want of something better to do, I grabbed Albert's new *Time* magazine to flip through.

I didn't get past the front cover text: "Brothers-In-Arms at Arms."

I stared at the words. As revelations so often do, it smacked me in the face when I wasn't even looking, my mind scrambling back over all I knew of Aroyan and Pavle Kasarian's personal histories. My thoughts kept returning to Albert's chuckle at the clue he'd given me: "Plain as day. In black and white." I'd assumed he meant the secret was obvious, not that it was actually written in black and white. No wonder he was so amused.

Skimming over the magazine title, the word *brothers* had grabbed my attention. Something in my subconscious must have caused me to seize upon it, because it was only after I turned its meaning over in my mind, played with it and massaged it, that small, seemingly inconsequential facts about Aroyan and the Kasarians began to collide then spin forward, painting a picture—illuminating an idea. Aroyan and Kasarian were not only brothers-in-arms but also half brothers.

Without all the research I'd done, I would have missed the connection. Hell, without the eidetic memory training, I probably wouldn't have figured it out. The clues were too widely placed. Too easily ignored or forgotten.

Pavle's charity was involved in the construction of the Olissan High Court building in Ulan. Designed to be the centerpiece of the city, the Olissan three-headed dragon, Zmey Gorynych, was etched into the front dome of curved bronze glass. I'd seen a press release on the building's ribbon cutting. Pavle had been visiting Ulan nine months before Aroyan's birth.

Aroyan's mother was a law secretary. She liked to husband hunt. Although married, Pavle was of royal blood and would have made enticing prey.

In the Aroyan biography, there'd been a picture of his mother at work. I hadn't put it together at the time, but she had to have been at the High Court.

The three dragonheads of Zmey Gorynych lurked in the background.

Although nothing I had was definitive, my gut told me I'd figured it out. I'd accepted Albert's challenge and conquered it. But now what?

15

"I'm seeing a lot of things I shouldn't," said Dagby from behind his desk. He tapped a pencil on his coffee cup then pointed to the TV screen. "Let's focus, people, or I may see fit to give you a pop quiz tomorrow."

At Dagby's request, a few people stopped their artistic endeavors, but most continued as if he had never spoken. I turned my attention back to the television. I didn't need to be in any more hot water with Dagby, who was currently sitting at his desk, checking he had received everyone's history reports. I'd watched him count through the stack. Then recount. Each time, he counted twenty-three reports instead of twenty-four. Dagby was making ticks in his attendance roster to find out who would get an earful about their missing assignment. I couldn't wait to be the lucky gal.

"...Vladik Kasarian is due to take office in two days. In a bold move, his opponent, Tarkan Aroyan, has filed a petition with the United Nations calling for a new election. This hit to the Kasarian camp comes on the heels of Alina Kasarian's outing of her employer, C-Fusion Corp, for illegal business dealings." Coming to the end of his report, Hunter looked relieved. "That's it for today's news report from Olissa. Tomorrow, I'll be coming to you from Ulan, the home city of Tarkan Aroyan. Please stay tuned for a special segment on Alina Kasarian by Galen Ostroff after these words from our sponsors."

Following advertisements for a zit cream and athletic shoes, Galen appeared on the screen. She was petite with freckles, glasses, and a blond pixie cut and sat behind a newsroom anchor desk.

"This is Galen Ostroff for Edunews. Over the last two weeks, Hunter Ludlow has been reporting from Olissa about the presidential campaign. Since coverage began, we've received an unprecedented number of emails from our viewers asking for more information about the enigmatic figure always at Vladik Kasarian's side, his sister, Alina."

Images of Alina flashed across the screen at Galen's right. Some were from her childhood, but the majority looked to be society page images from just prior to her accident. In them, Alina wore designer dresses and struck poses for the camera. She must have been in her teens, but she looked far younger—like a child dressed up in her mother's clothes.

"Alina's is a story equally as intriguing as her brother's. Prior to the helicopter crash Alina survived at the age of twenty, she was a budding socialite and well-known figure in the Paris and Zurich social circuits. Although Alina has given few personal interviews since the accident, we were able to find an interview given to her college newspaper. In it, she shares freely her thoughts on life both before and after that near-fatal crash."

Galen disappeared as a picture of Alina in a wheelchair came onto the screen and stayed. She was bent over her books and looked to be in a library. A bodiless voice with an Olissan accent began to speak—a voice-over translation of Alina's words.

"Before the accident, I had no direction. My brother was the family's future. No one cared what I did with myself, and so I did nothing of import. I partied. I played. But with the accident, I realized how precious life is. It changed me for the better. I may be scarred. I may be unable to walk, but I would much rather be who I am now than who I was before. Now, I'm a physicist focusing on alternative energies. With my current research into cold fusion, I'm hoping my brother won't be the only one in our family making a significant contribution to society."

Galen came back on the screen. I looked around the room as she spoke. Instead of doodling or passing notes, most of the class was finally paying attention. In fact, Dagby was the only one not watching the screen. I found him staring at me. He pointed at the clock and then at his desk. The bell was about to ring, and I took his gesture to mean I was to stay after. I nodded and turned my attention back to Galen.

"In the interview, Alina goes on to talk about how the accident not only changed her outlook on the world, but also brought her closer to her brother," said Galen.

Another image of Alina appeared on the screen. This time she was with her brother and they were in a laboratory at C-Fusion Corp.

"Before the accident, Vladik never had much use for me. He was always a serious boy, and I was his frivolous sister. We hadn't seen each other or spoken in five years. But now. Now, we're close. We're bonded by the loss of our parents and our hopes for a better Olissa and a better world."

Galen returned to the screen. "As we approach year six of

the Middle East War with blackouts wreaking havoc on the US economy and gas prices continuing to rise, perhaps it will be Alina Kasarian and her research into cold fusion that quiets the world's demand for energy. Next up, Zachary Wayne is in Saudi Arabia to report on the synchronized plaza bombings in the capital cities of Saudi Arabia, Kuwait, and Bahrain."

The bell rang and jolted everyone's attention away from the television. I waited at my desk as people packed up and filed out. I felt a closeness to Alina and sat wondering what it was like to be her. We'd each had a life that was taken away from us. And perhaps I'd been given a better life just as she had.

"So Lex, why don't I have your paper?" asked Dagby, interrupting my meditations.

"I'm really sorry, Mr. D, but I didn't finish. I had the most horrible menstrual cramps last night. I felt terrible. Really, really bad," I said, deciding to go with the crimson tide excuse, as it tended to work so well.

Despite the intriguing soap opera of it all, Aroyan and Kasarian being brothers wasn't something I could write about. I had no hard and fast evidence. All I had were pieces of a puzzle that fit together and aligned with Albert's clues. I couldn't base a paper on his assurances. According to Albert, the CIA had discovered the relationship through blood samples—evidence I could hardly reference in a bibliography—but didn't know much else. They weren't even sure if Vladik Kasarian knew he was Aroyan's half brother. Then there was the problem of Dagby possibly believing my assertions. He wouldn't smack an *A* on my paper and hand it back, but would make a big deal out of it, possibly calling in local media. The last thing I needed was to have my photo splashed across the papers. After tarnishing Aroyan's image, a man Perun was no doubt backing, I'd be the walking dead as far as Perun was concerned.

In a way, I wished I could write about it, as it fit Dagby's assignment so perfectly. It made good sense why Aroyan was keeping the secret. He was campaigning as an everyman made good through hard work, and having royal Kasarian blood didn't suit that image. There's also the chance his motivations would have been questioned. As a prominent businessman with no previous history in politics, his sudden foray into the political arena was surprising. If people knew of his blood relationship to Vladik and that Pavle Kasarian had all but forsaken his bastard son, the public might have believed Aroyan's sudden involvement in politics was motivated by something other than his idealistic convictions. The campaign had been a dirty one, after all. Then again, if spun in the right way, the secret could have hurt the Kasarian family. An abandoned illegitimate child doesn't do wonders for the family image. There's no telling what might have happened had the secret been common knowledge, and I would have had fun coming up with different scenarios.

Mr. Dagby's brow furrowed with sympathy at hearing of my menstrual woes. "I'm really sorry to hear that, Lex. Did you try a hot water bottle or some Pamprin? The ads for Pamprin say it's good for period relief, not just pain relief."

"I took some Advil," I said, trying to hide my astonishment at having finally met a man unintimidated by a period.

"Maybe give the Pamprin a try next time. When do you think you'll be able to get the report to me? I know you have the homecoming game and the dance. Do you think Monday would work?"

I nodded. "Thanks so much, Mr. D. That's really nice of you."

He smiled. "My wife taught me to be sensitive about female issues. She had terrible cramps until menopause. Now it's hot flashes. But please don't tell your classmates. I'd hate for others to take advantage of me." Dagby nodded toward the television. "So what do you think about Aroyan petitioning for a new election?"

My phone chimed with a text just as I was formulating an answer. I glanced down at the display to find a jumble of letters—a modified Caesar cipher.

LMUGCACGTMBIGNHQJENLOJO

"I don't know," I said, my mind focused on deciphering the code.

O-R-C-H

"I personally don't understand why he's fighting so hard. He's spending his fortune on the campaign and fighting the United States, but his companies have profited greatly from our presence in Olissa. The United States is one of his main buyers. I'd think he'd want us to stay."

"Maybe his ideals mean more to him than money?"

I-D-H-O-U-S

"Well, statistics show quality of life has markedly improved since the US settled in."

"Sorry, what did you just say?"

E-N-O-O-N-T-O

"When I was visiting, the people seemed happy. The rebuild was almost complete and—"

M-O-R-R-O-W

I walked out of Dagby's classroom a few minutes later with a nauseating pit in my stomach. Another meet with Mistress could mean nothing good.

Grant fell into step beside me a few seconds later and took my hand with a smile. "Hey," he said, nudging me with his shoulder. "Want to hang out tonight after football practice?"

An excuse for why I couldn't hang out immediately came to mind. Although I'd started the day being a most excellent girlfriend—baked goods were involved—I wondered if tomorrow wouldn't be better for starting fresh. Maybe after my meeting with Mistress was over, I'd be able to focus. "Grant, I..."

I stopped myself. In front of me, Tiff Harms was plastering a new bumper sticker on her locker. YOLO it said in bold black letters—You Only Live Once.

Y-O-L-O

The four letters taunted me.

Grab ahold bitch, and let it ride, they said. *LET IT RIDE.*

It was a cliché but a good one.

I grabbed Grant's hand and tugged him forward. Caught off guard, he didn't move fast enough, so I pulled harder.

"Lex, what are you doing?"

I pulled Grant into an empty classroom and closed the door. "Yeah, let's hang out tonight. I'd love to," I said, pushing Grant against a nearby wall.

We locked eyes for a moment, then my lips found his.

Mint and oranges.

No longer lagging behind, one of Grant's hands snaked through my hair, pulling me deeper into the kiss. Electricity coiled down my spine.

I sunk into the moment, letting sensation overtake me—goose bumps, tingling, fire. For once, I let myself, without guilt, revel in the truth that comes with the rise of our animal senses. Senses not ruled by the mind.

Grant and I had a connection. I could build up as many emotional walls as I wanted, but he kept sneaking past every one of them.

16

With mixed emotions, I headed back to the orchid house. As drizzle morphed into a full-on downpour, I flipped my hood up to guard against the rain and tried to distract myself by thinking of the day ahead with the big football game and homecoming dance. Fun awaited me, and all I needed to do was get through the meeting with Mistress first.

With the increased threat level, I'd expected my orders to be rescinded when I deciphered the Caesar. While I was happy to be back in the Perun fold, I was nervous about being beckoned to another meeting. As a high school student, I was in a position of little strategic value, and the only reason for being called—that I could fathom—had to do with Varos. They either wanted to pump me for more information or somehow use me as bait to bring him out of hiding.

My phone chimed as I neared the orchid house and a message from Martine popped up.

ur going to luv the dress I picked 4 u. Va va voom.

After the football game, Martine and I, along with her girlfriend, Sadie, were getting together to prep for our respective homecoming dances. With everything going on in my life, I hadn't found time to shop, and Martine was loaning me a dress. I laughed at seeing her message, hoping she hadn't picked something that showed too much cleavage.

As I returned the cell to my pocket, a gust of strong wind swept across the park, driving the rain horizontal. I turned my head away from the icy bite of it, and it was then I caught a whiff of cologne. Someone was close. The rain had masked the sound of their approach and, limiting my peripheral vision, the hood I wore blocked them from view. I zigged to the right and turned, bringing up my hands for defense. Catching a flash of someone lunging toward me, I threw an elbow into the air and caught the person in the face. I narrowly missed a full-body tackle. As it was, Okan knocked my purse away, relieving me of my gun.

"Milena. So careless. I almost had you," said Okan, regaining his footing. He touched his split lip then licked at the blood and smiled. Okan wore a black Adidas tracksuit and diamond studs in both ears. My old enemy from Perun now looked like a low-level thug—a wannabe rapper with a nostril-flaring problem.

My skin crawled at seeing him, but at the same time, I wanted to laugh. He looked so ridiculous. "Only one of us is bleeding," I countered. I glanced at my purse, but it was too far away.

Okan smirked, wiping a hand across his bloody nose. "You always had more luck than skill. I'm glad the mission's no longer in your hands. A "Necessary" should have never been chosen for something so important, despite what Mistress said. Nice cheer-leading uniform, by the way. Ra Ra. Go team."

"So I'm to stand down?" I asked, trying to sound unperturbed despite being worried Perun had learned of my betrayal. Why else would Okan attack? Did they somehow know I'd gotten rid of the poison, or worse still, did they think I'd informed on them to Albert, causing the change in threat level?

"Yep, you're on stand down until further notice," said Okan, putting his guard up and moving toward me at speed.

He threw a punch. I dodged and he got air. This seemed to piss him off, because after that he came at me hard, throwing punch after punch. Some of his punches landed, but many were glancing blows as I was able to keep out of range. I darted in for a few quick blows of my own, landing an upper cut to his jaw and a front kick to his abdomen.

It was during my second front kick that Okan managed to grab hold of my leg. As he pulled up, trying to dump me on my butt, I bent my leg and grabbed the front of his shirt. I took him down with me, and we landed in a messy heap, Okan on top. My aim had been to catapult him over my head with my bent leg, but things hadn't gone to plan. The dude was hiding some serious heft under his ridiculous getup.

Okan grabbed for my throat and took a firm hold. "Such a stupid move. Now look where you are."

I could tell from the smile on Okan's face that he was only meaning to play with me, not kill me. I looked at Okan with what I hoped was calmness in my face and popped the button on the sheath holding my knife. My cheerleading uniform didn't allow for a concealed weapon, so I'd stowed the knife in my jacket pocket.

"Already given up?" asked Okan, when I didn't immediately try to break free. His grip began to loosen.

"Already won," I retorted, pulling the knife free and bringing it to where he could feel it, resting near his groin.

Okan was off me in seconds. "*Suka*," he spat, reverting to Oline.

I stood slowly, keeping the knife in my hand and a wary eye on Okan. "So what was this little sparring match about?"

Okan laughed. "Just me enjoying myself. Making sure you hadn't gone all soft. We need to keep the merchandise in tip-top shape."

"So it wasn't Mistress I was supposed to meet?" I asked, brushing dirt and leaves off my coat and skirt.

Okan shook his head no and leered.

"What do you want?" I asked, touching my cheek gingerly. "Do you have any idea how stupid you are for bruising me? Now I'll have to come up with some excuse for why I look like a freak show. This better be worth it." I glanced at my watch. If I didn't hurry, I wouldn't have time to go home and put on another uniform. Thanks to Okan's pissing match, what I wore was stained with dirt.

"Varos," said Okan. "He's gone to ground and has been causing problems. I'm in charge of finding him. What do you know?"

"Oh my God," I said, widening my eyes and trying to sound surprised and concerned by the news. "What's he been doing?" I motioned for Okan to follow me as I returned to my car.

"Varos has been playing with air traffic control radar, screwing with the police, messing with TV network broadcasts—it's all undirected action. He's basically being a spoiled brat and we can't reach him."

I stopped and turned to Okan, pointing the knife at him. "You're lying. Varos would never do those things. Perun might, but not Varos on his own. What's he really been doing?"

Okan grinned. "I'm impressed, Milena. I never did understand why Mistress was so enthralled with you, but maybe she was right. Maybe you are a fox."

I resumed walking, swiping with irritation at the wet hair plastered to my cheeks. *Enthralled with me? Was Okan blind and deaf?*

"He's been messing with the covers of Perun operatives. Changing grades for those at universities. Hacking bank accounts. Yesterday, he issued an arrest warrant for one of our operatives in California. The guy was pulled out of the office and charged with being a kiddie fiddler."

Exasperated, I stopped and pointed the knife again. "Quit lying. He would never endanger any of us."

Okan arched an eyebrow and laughed. He walked forward until the tip of my knife touched his sternum. "I'm not lying," said Okan, coming to within inches of my face. He ran a finger along the edge of my knife, drawing his own blood.

I jammed my foot down on his toes and pushed him back with my free hand, annoyed by his attempt at playing the badass. "When did he go missing?" I asked, trying to wrap my head around the fact Okan might not actually be lying. My brain kept returning to a single question. *Why would Varos betray us?*

"Three weeks ago. Dropped off the grid. No one's been able to find him. He's clearly gone insane. Some people just can't hack the pressure."

"Hmmm," I said, pondering just how irritated I wanted to make Okan. It took only seconds for me to decide on pretty damn irritated, as I was feeling defensive on Varos's behalf. Okan had to be lying about Varos. I did not, for one second, believe he had lost his marbles. "I think I'd rather talk to Mistress about this. You've proven yourself to be less than the finest Perun has to offer."

Okan gave an appreciative laugh. "Well. Well. Well. What a vindictive little bitch you've become." Okan darted forward and began walking backward. He raised a speculative eyebrow. "I wonder how second rate your boyfriend, Grant, would find my skills? Think he could take me?" Okan halted abruptly. "I'm thinkin' not."

I zigged around Okan. "He's nothing to me. Do what you want," I said with a nonchalant shrug, hoping like hell Okan couldn't see his words scared me half to death. At hearing the threat, my heart rate had surged uncomfortably, making it physically painful to act calm.

"Come on. Quit being a bitch."

I stuck my hands into my pockets and shrugged again, as if what I knew about Varos was insignificant. "He was acting tired before his disappearance and was more disheveled than usual but nothing terribly out of the ordinary. He sometimes got that way. I always assumed it was because he was busy with a mission."

I needed to tell Okan something. Pretending everything was completely normal would have raised a red flag. Okan was undoubtedly talking to the other cadets Varos handled. Still, I couldn't keep myself from playing with Okan a little bit. "I might have a way for you to contact him, but it's a long shot."

"Tell me," said Okan, jogging forward and then falling in line at my side.

"Back at the compound, Varos was a big fan of Johnny Knoxville and *Jackass* from back in the day. He would visit message boards—"

"*Vzzzt*," said Okan, cutting me off. "Try again, we didn't have internet access."

I shot him a look. "Varos had access. Trust me. He visited a lot of *Jackass* message boards. Varos liked to call me Little O. It was for Odile, a nickname I had before Perun. I'm not sure if he still visits them, but maybe if you log on as Odile and allude to being in some sort of trouble, he'll contact you."

"That sounds like the longest of long shots."

"It's all I got."

17

Outside Martine's house, I peered out my front windshield at the rain coming down. Had my old friend gone rogue and turned against Perun? Running was one thing, but betraying other cadets was something else entirely. It was unforgiveable. I knew Okan wasn't someone to trust, but the look in his eyes as he stood pressed against my knife worried me. I needed to talk with Varos and find out for myself what was really going on.

Knowing Varos as I did, I figured he'd be monitoring Okan's internet usage. He'd helped design the network used by Perun's leadership, the handlers, and active operatives, so he had the capabilities. *Tracking the person tracking you* was classic Varos, and I hoped he would get my message via Okan as my other attempt at contacting him seemed to have failed. Only recently activated and with a mission meant to land me in prison, it was unfortunate I'd never been cleared to access the network myself. At Perun, Varos regularly referred to Okan as a jackass, hence sending him to a Johnny Knoxville message board, and Odile was the black swan in Swan Lake—Odette's evil doppelganger. By using the name Odile, Varos would know I was the one who had sent Okan looking in that direction, and I hoped he would contact me as a result.

From my car, I could see Martine and Sadie dancing around

in Martine's bedroom. I sucked in a long, deep breath as I watched them, then another. With everything that was going on in my spy life, I was finding it harder and harder to switch into high school mode, but I wanted to appreciate having Alexandra's life while I could. I now knew how easily it could be taken away.

The rain was coming down in a torrent when I finally jumped from my car. Already soaked from the game, which had gone into two overtimes, I wasn't worried about getting wet. At least we'd won in the end, thanks to a Hail Mary pass from Grant in the last five seconds. Grant was now on top of the world. Before I left him, he'd picked me up, swung me around, and said three words that nearly made my heart stop. "I love you."

In an instant, he'd moved past "a college nearby" to something far more significant. And I wasn't prepared. Not by a long shot. I'd found his mouth for a kiss but said nothing. I felt both dread and delight at his words and couldn't separate the two. Grant may have meant those words, but that didn't make them true. He loved my façade of Alexandra but not me. Would he have been interested if I wasn't popular? If I wasn't a cheerleader? If I hadn't been orphaned? Would he have loved my actual face? What about my smile and laugh? Did I even have these true bits of myself to show him anymore? Could I muster up my old smile and laugh if asked? Part of me doubted I was capable. Would he have loved the gnarled feet of the ballet dancer I'd hoped to be? Would he have understood that passion?

Still, it had been nice to hear the words, even if I knew they weren't really true. I wanted Alexandra's life, after all. After almost losing it, I knew wholeheartedly I wanted it. I wanted to make it mine and wondered if maybe I could slowly put more of myself into it, nothing drastic, but just something more. A few bits here and there so Grant and Albert could get to know me more. Grant and I had an undeniable chemistry. It was something that ran deep, and I wondered if maybe he really could love me if given the chance.

Amélie, Martine's grandmother, opened the door before I had a chance to knock. "Come in *ma chérie*, Martine is upstairs with Sa… Oh my, what happened to your face?"

"I tripped while reading a text and face-planted. It wasn't one of my finer moments."

"Oh my," said Amélie again, her hand coming to my bruised cheek. "Don't worry, I'll fix it so you can't even see. I'll go get my makeup."

I trudged upstairs as Amélie scurried off. Martine peeked around her door at hearing my approach and stuck out her camera, snapping my picture. Her fluorescent red hair was gone, replaced by her natural black but with dark blue highlights. "I thought you'd never get here. Sadie and I are dying to see you in THE DRESS."

"Love the new hair," I said, entering her room.

"It's for that dinner with my dad. The blue's more subdued than the red." As Martine spoke, her eyes drifted up and down my bedraggled form. "Lex, what the hell happened to your face? Your cheek's purple."

I moved past Martine and plonked myself down on the floor, giving Sadie a wave as I went splat. "I wiped out while reading your text this morning. Apparently, I can't do two things at once."

"Martine, it's all your fault. You're such a bully," said Sadie with a laugh.

Sadie was five-foot-nothing with a mop of curly red hair that would make Medusa proud. Unlike Martine with her punk flair, Sadie looked like a sophisticated artist type. Both she and Martine loved fashion, but while Martine was edgy and provocative, Sadie was all about timelessness and clean, crisp lines. On the surface, Sadie and Martine seemed like an odd couple, but somehow, they worked well together.

"Hah, hah, hah," said Martine, blowing Sadie a kiss with her middle finger.

Sadie gasped and grabbed the kiss, stuffing it in her back pocket as if to hide the impropriety of it away.

Despite being soaked, exhausted, and bruised, I couldn't help but laugh. Sadie and Martine were too cute sometimes. A perfect match.

"All right, we better stop messing around," said Sadie. "We need to get started. Especially since Miss Clutzo is going to need some work."

Martine skipped over to a garment bag hanging on the closet door. "This is your dress." Like a magician's assistant, she slowly unzipped the garment bag and then whipped the dress out. "Voilà."

My eyes widened. The black dress shimmered as the room's light played off the crystal beading. It was a form-fitting, high-collar dress, with a provocative slit.

"Wow," I said. "That's gorgeous. Are you sure you want to loan it to me? It looks like a dress for the Oscars, not a piddly homecoming dance."

"It's Gram's. And she wore it to the Cesar Awards back when she lived in France. I think she wore it when she was twenty or something crazy like that. She suggested it for you. Neither Sadie nor I could ever hope to get into this puppy."

At that moment, Amélie walked into the room, carrying her makeup bag. She paused at seeing the dress and smiled. "It has only been worn the once. I hope it serves you well tonight."

"Come on, let's get this dress on you in case we need to do alterations," said Martine, bouncing up and down.

The girls had me out of my wet clothes and stepping into the dress in seconds. Amélie zipped me up in back then led me over to the full-length mirror hanging on the closet. "*Ma chérie, c'est parfait.*" Amélie took my hand in hers. "It is perfect, no?"

I glanced down at the dress's fine beading. "Wow, I feel incredible in this." I turned to look at the back. The dress fit like a glove, accentuating all my positive attributes. I heard the *click, click, click* of a camera shutter as Martine snapped more pictures. I turned and struck a model's pose, being careful to hide my bruised cheek.

Amélie pulled a picture out of her pocket and handed it to me after Martine and I were done. "This was me in the dress at the Cesars. The actor, Henri Merteuil, was my beau at the time."

Amélie had been a stunner in her youth. In the picture, her thick black hair was cut in a chin-length bob with blunt-cut bangs. Her hair suited the dress, which oozed elegance. The photographer had captured Amélie laughing while draped on the arm of Henri, and Henri smiling down at her in adoration. "Compared to you, I don't do this dress justice," I said, passing the picture to Sadie.

I studied my image in the mirror. I didn't see any of the joie de vivre so apparent in the photograph. "Amélie. You said once you used to cut hair?"

She nodded. "Back in France."

"How 'bout giving it another go. I need a change, and that bob of yours looks pretty amazing."

Both Amélie and Martine's faces lit up.

"That's a brilliant idea," said Martine, grabbing for her camera again.

Amélie clapped her hands together in delight and giggled. "*Ma chérie*, this is going to be so much fun."

18

Sitting in the far corner of the auditorium, I watched with envy as my fellow classmates bobbed up and down to Rihanna's newest single. After the fun I'd had at Martine's getting ready, and feeling like a million bucks with the new haircut and dress, I couldn't wait to get out there. To celebrate keeping my life as Alexandra, I'd vowed to let myself have fun—at least for the night, but instead of doing just that, I was waiting at a table for Grant to return and explain himself.

I knew something was off with Grant as soon as he'd picked me up for the dance. I received only a quick peck on the cheek, and nothing was said of my dress or hair. Normally, Grant would have bombarded me with compliments. During our big group dinner, he had smiled and even cracked a few jokes, but I still sensed something was off. His smiles weren't reaching his eyes, and he was ignoring me, instead focusing on everyone else. Questions I asked were answered with only a word or two. Others wouldn't have noticed his change in behavior, but I certainly did. It was a far cry from the "I love you" I'd received on the football field.

The dance was already in full swing when our group arrived fashionably late. Wanting a memento from the night, I'd asked Grant to get a picture taken with me. He'd agreed somewhat grudgingly.

As we stood side by side under the balloon archway, Grant mumbled something about "not being able to take it anymore." Instead of heading to the dance floor, Grant grabbed my hand and ushered me away from the action so we could talk. Reaching the corner farthest from all the fun, we sat. Grant said nothing at first, instead choosing to try and stare me down, his eyes showing a steeliness I hadn't seen before. Finally, he sighed, shook his head, and stood. "I'm going to get us some punch."

I wanted to yell at him to rip off the damn Band-Aid, but something inside kept me quiet. Perhaps it was that Grant had always been more than patient with me.

Returning, Grant thrust a glass at me. I took it and, suddenly feeling very parched, gulped it down. "Thanks," I said, offering a smile.

Grant only nodded as he drained his glass and sat back down. He sighed again, then looked to the ceiling as if asking God for strength. "We need to talk."

"What's up?" I asked, running a hand over his leg.

Grant grabbed it roughly and held it still.

"You're not going to get away with not talking by working me with your feminine wiles." Grant's eyes were hard and locked on mine. Unconsciously, his thumb began to slide back and forth over the scar on my wrist.

I blinked, then smiled. "Feminine wiles? Have you been reading Jane Austen again?" I pulled my arm away and covered the scar with my hand.

Grant frowned. "You've been running me in circles, and I'm tired of it. We're going to talk. No funny business. No jokes."

I turned away and looked out at the mass of gyrating bodies. Rihanna was gone, replaced by Justin. "All right then. Talk."

"You're not acting like yourself, and you haven't been for weeks. I want to know what's going on."

Wanting Grant's trust, I made a point to find his eyes. "I have no idea what you're talking about. Of course I've been acting like myself. Who else would I be acting like?"

"Your hair. Your dress. You look great, but these aren't you. And I saw you taking swigs from Dave's flask in the car. Since when do you drink?"

"Everyone likes to play dress up." I tried to find a smile for Grant but came up empty, my mouth twisting itself into a frown. "This dress and the hair. It's no big deal. And so what if I had a few sips from the flask. It's our senior year. I'm just trying to have fun for once. We'll never be able to come back to this. I don't want to miss out."

"What about challenging Dave to *Espionage 4*? You hate video games. Last time I suggested a video game date at The Gamespot, you shot me down. Hard. So what's that about?"

And this was why I didn't drink. Drinking makes you sloppy. I shrugged, trying to hide how uncomfortable I was feeling under Grant's harsh glare. "I saw it advertised on TV and thought it looked fun. I wanted to get it for Albert since he's CIA, a gag gift since he's an analyst, but thought it might be good to try it out first. So it's no grand conspiracy, okay?"

Grant stared at me again, searching for something. For once, I'd been trying to let loose and be more genuine, and now Grant was actually calling me on it. Feeling nervous, I babbled on. "I'm seventeen, who's to say who the real me is? Or the real you? Or—"

"You've been lying. Skipping school. That's not you."

A slow song began, and I glanced back at the dance floor. The mass of gyrating bodies quieted as partners found each other and began to sway. *Why wasn't I out there? Why wasn't Grant pulling me close and tucking his hands into the small of my back? Why weren't his lips brushing my ear and whispering something sweet?*

I'd thought through so many different scenarios for how the dance was going to go. They'd all been fun and highly romantic, like we were the leads in a movie. Lots of laughing and kissing and meaningful touches. None of the scenarios included anything like this. I shook my head, exasperated. "I had cramps for God's sake. Cut me some slack."

Grant clenched his jaw and shook his head. "We've been dating for a year and a half. I may not like to talk about it, but I'm pretty sure your period only comes once a month, and judging from the mood swings, I'd say you're a first-of-the-month kind of girl. You skipped school to go who the hell knows where, and you lied about going to UVA."

"What? No, I didn't. And my cycle's totally irregular. I saw a doctor about it, and he wanted to put me on birth control but that freaked my grandfather out, so I—"

"Ryan Gold," spat Grant.

"The field goal kicker?"

"We got to talking about colleges after the game. Turns out he went to UVA the same day as you for a visit. Only he didn't see you."

I rolled my eyes. "It's a big campus. We must have missed

each other."

"You said you grabbed the nine a.m. bus, which is the one Ryan took. You said you took the campus tour at eleven, which is the tour he took." Grant's eyes were boring into me; they were mad but also sad. "Why did you lie to me? What are you up to?"

My stomach churned uncomfortably at seeing his distress. I took his hand in mine and leaned in to kiss his cheek then wrapped my arms around him. My mind was scrambling for another lie to tell. A lie to cover my lie. In that moment, it seemed like all I ever did was lie. Liar, liar, pants on fire.

Finally, my mind grabbed onto something. It was a bad lie. One I didn't like. One I didn't want to use. I threw it away, searching for something else, but nothing better came. My lies about the video game and my period had come so easily. They'd slid off my tongue as if they were truths. But not this time. The seconds ticked by.

"I'm sorry I lied. It was such a stupid thing to lie about," I said, still scrambling.

"Then why'd you do it?" whispered Grant.

I ran my fingers through his hair. I had nothing to say. Nothing good, anyway.

Not wanting to speak, I cleared my throat. "I...I...I spent the day at my parent's graves... I didn't tell you because I didn't want you to have to think of your mom. I know how sad it makes you." I could feel Grant tense at the mention of his mother, and I hugged him tighter, wanting to take his pain away. "It's just when my birthday comes around, it reminds me of the life I had before they died. I look at the little girl in my photos, and it reminds me of the life she was supposed to have. And, I don't know... I just wanted to talk to them for a while. You understand…don't you?"

Heartbeats passed…and nothing happened. More heartbeats. I ached for something to happen, anything. Then Grant began to stroke my back, a tender caress. With a sigh, I laid my head on his shoulder. I hadn't wanted to use that lie, but it had worked. Once again I'd bamboozled my boyfriend. The thought made me sick. My heart wilted.

"You know how it changes you," I continued, trying to give Grant something that was true. "When your Mom died, it made you strong. You seized life. You tried out for the football team. You asked me out. You stopped hiding in the corners. When my parents died, that's when I started hiding. I'm only finding myself now."

"I'm sorry, Lex. I should have known it was something like that, but you need to quit protecting me. I'm not a kid."

In that moment, all I wanted was to be a normal girl with normal problems. With every fiber of my being, I wanted to stop being deceitful. Having to keep track of so many stories was exhausting. I realized then something had shifted when I'd chosen Albert over Perun. Even though Albert was safe and I was back in the Perun fold, something felt different. I needed more of the real me in my life.

I pulled away from the hug. "Grant, you're going to think this is really strange and coming out of nowhere, but I was wondering if…well, if maybe…you'd be interested in taking a ballroom dance class with me? It might be a fun activ—"

Grant laughed. "You're joking, right?" He pulled back farther and looked at me cockeyed. "With these two left feet? I look like

I'm having a seizure when I dance, which is okay for something like this"—Grant gestured to the dance floor—"but not for ballroom."

My already wilted heart shriveled down to nothing. I was hollow.

The microphone squawked, breaking the awkward silence between us. We turned as Laura James took the stage. "Hope everyone is having a great time tonight. The votes have now been counted, and it's time to announce the results of our homecoming race." Laura paused to undo the envelope then smiled. "Well, it seems the race wasn't even close this year." Laura scanned the room and finding Grant and I, she pointed in our direction. "This year's homecoming king and queen are…Grant Horne and—"

I flinched as she said "Alexandra Gastone."

Laura raised her hands into the air and began to clap. As if in unison, the room moved their collective attention to our remote corner.

Grant turned to me and smiled. For the first time that night, the smile reached his eyes. "We won. Can you believe it?" With a renewed sense of enthusiasm for the night, Grant hopped up and pulled me to standing. "Come on," said Grant, tugging me toward the stage. He waved to the crowd as we walked. Everyone continued to clap. The DJ found a pop version of "God Save The Queen" and it began to blast across the speakers.

For the blood of the fallen…

I no longer had any urge to join the crowd, so I stumbled along blindly behind Grant. I'd just lied to his face for the umpteenth time. Everything around me, every word I spoke, was a lie. I didn't deserve a crown. I didn't deserve people's applause. I'd dug up dirt on dozens in the room, and depending on future circumstances, I might need to use what I had against them.

For the blood of the living...

Grant towed me up onto the stage and then made a great show of kneeling as Laura placed the crown on his head and handed him the scepter. He stood, raising the scepter high. The football team roared in response. The music blared, making me wince.

I looked out at the crowd, trying to hold my emotions in check. It all felt wrong. Very, very wrong.

For Olissa we fight...

Somehow the crown found my head, and Laura jabbed in a few bobby pins.

"Smile," said Grant, taking my hand.

I did as instructed, peeling the sides of my mouth up and showing some teeth. Grant kissed my cheek and then, with great fanfare, dipped me backward.

The crowd began to laugh.

Then the lights went out.

19

"Lex, are you almost ready?" hollered Albert. "We need to get going if we're going to pick up Grant on time."

"Five more minutes," I yelled back, as I leaned into the mirror, mascara wand in hand. Inspired by my new hairdo, I was pulling out all the stops for my evening out with my two favorite men. We were celebrating a week early because Albert had a work engagement the following weekend, and I finally felt like I had a right to enjoy the day. I couldn't remember my actual birthdate and had decided to claim the day as my own. The awkwardness of the homecoming dance was behind me—thank you blackout—and I vowed not to think of it again. I had emotionally distanced myself from Perun in order to help Albert. It was going to take some time to get my head back in the right place. I still believed in the cause and that it was worth the sacrifices. I was living a lie for a very important reason, and it was an honor to have been chosen. I just needed to get some perspective back. And so what if my first attempt at sharing more of the real me with Grant failed. I'd just need to ease him into it. Maybe start with something smaller than a dance class.

Finished with my eyes, I dabbed on some lip gloss and ran a brush through my hair. At my full-length mirror, I gave myself the once-over, paying particular attention to my bruised cheek. The concealer I'd applied rather generously seemed to be doing its job.

I didn't look half bad. My ensemble was black. Black leather miniskirt, black cashmere sweater, black tights, black knee-high boots. The one thing that would have made the outfit perfect was my locket, but I still hadn't found it. I'd checked at school and the cyber café and come up empty.

"How do I look?" I asked, turning in Ork's direction. He lifted one of his brows then let out an excited *woof, woof, woof.* I took his excitement as a "You go girl."

I snagged my black purse off the bed and then did a quick spin, searching for my car keys. Three people couldn't fit comfortably in Albert's XKE, so tonight we'd be riding in style in my truck. I spotted my keys sitting next to a polished oak box on my dresser, containing Albert's birthday present to me—a Glock 17, Gen4. Although Albert was a gun aficionado and we went to the firing range from time to time, the gift felt like a strange one as I'd never shown any real interest in firearms. Albert's gifts were usually very thoughtful, and I wondered what I'd done to suggest I might want a gun. Was it Albert's way of recognizing I was an adult now and legal to carry? Did it have to do with his CIA background that he thought I would want such a thing? Was the fact I was a spy causing me to overthink the gift? Probably.

Not wanting to think about the gun or see it when I returned, I grabbed it and stuffed it into a drawer. Out of sight, out of mind.

"Tonight is going to be a good night. A nice, uneventful night," I mumbled to myself as I turned out the bedroom light.

I was halfway down the stairs when I called out to Albert. "All right, Grandpa. You got the tickets? I'm ready to rock and—"

"Surprise!" yelled Albert and a small, tidy group behind him.

Taken off guard at the sight of Martine and Amélie, I took a misstep and fell backward, skidding a couple of steps before regaining my footing.

"Wow," I said, pasting a smile on my face. "Just, wow. When did everyone get here? I didn't hear a thing."

"When you were in the shower," said Albert, walking up to take my hand. He kissed my cheek then walked me the rest of the way down.

"Wow," I said again, at a loss for words. Wanting an answer as to why two people I'd never once mentioned to Albert were at my birthday party, I wrapped Albert in a hug. To our guests, it would look like I was simply being affectionate with my grandfather, but really I wanted to throttle him. "How?" I asked.

I could feel Albert begin to laugh before the sound of it reached my ears. "Lex, I am in the CIA. I do have my ways."

Albert tried to pull back from the hug, but I wouldn't let him go. "And what ways would those be?"

Albert's laughter stopped abruptly as he sensed my growing anger. "Amélie called our landline last week. She wanted to invite us over for dinner." Albert wrenched himself free and turned me toward the room. "I know you didn't want anything big, so I kept it small. Just your boyfriend and best friend. I also have my own date," said Albert, nodding to Amélie. "I hope you don't mind?"

I raised an eyebrow and looked at Albert, who then winked at me. Why couldn't he have kept things simple? I liked simple. Grant couldn't take his eyes off Martine. She was another secret I'd been keeping from him, a secret with blue highlights and a unique personal style. I was sure she was unlike anyone Grant had ever met. Martine was my secret friend. The kind of person I would have surrounded myself with if I were Milena Rokva. She wasn't meant to be in Alexandra's life. She wasn't meant to meet Alexandra's boyfriend. I wanted to share more with Grant, but I doubted I would have shared Martine. If he didn't like her, then I'd have known, without a doubt, he wouldn't like the real me.

"The limo's outside," said Albert. "We should probably leave now in order to make our dinner reservation. After dinner, we have tickets to the Alvin Ailey dancers for eight o'clock."

"Limo?" I asked. "And Alvin Ailey?" I knew Albert didn't particularly like dance. He'd taken me to The Nutcracker and had fallen asleep.

Albert smiled. "I can't have my date riding around in that old clunker of yours, and I thought we should do something cultured for the evening. Grant and I discussed our choices and came up with Alvin Ailey."

"I saw you looking at the advertisement in the newspaper," chimed Grant.

My head toggled between Albert and Grant in disbelief. A night of dance was the perfect gift. It was sheer luck it was happening, but I'd take it. I'd take it and pretend it was because Albert and Grant knew me so well. I'd give myself that fantasy for the evening, and maybe, just maybe, I would survive unscathed, my two worlds colliding. Grant wouldn't do the ballroom dance classes, but he would take me to see dance, which was something. A step in the right direction.

The limo ride into the city was blessedly short and uneventful.

Albert regaled everyone with stories of my previous birthdays. The man could make anything sound exciting, which was saying something considering he was talking about hayrides and painting pottery. Although I was still angry with Albert for inviting Martine and Amélie, I was starting to mellow by the end of the ride.

At D & G's, we were taken to a private room and seated. Albert handed the waiter two bottles for uncorking, one of wine and one of sparkling cider, and after the waiter's departure, he took the wine bottle and poured everyone a glass.

"I have a few things to say in honor of Lex's birthday," said Albert, raising a glass. "As you all may know, Lex isn't one for birthday celebrations. For her, tonight is probably more about pleasing me. But each year on her birthday, I thank God he saved that little girl I met in Prague and saw fit to put her in my charge. Each day with Lex has been a blessing. Happy eighteenth birthday!"

"Cheers," said the table, everyone leaning in to clink glasses.

I smiled bashfully and followed suit, wiping a stray tear from my eye. I took a sip then raised my glass in Albert's direction mouthing a "thank you."

The toast done, Martine handed me a small package. "It's from both me and Grams."

"Happy birthday, *ma chérie*," said Amélie.

"Thank you," I said, undoing the wrapping. "You didn't need to get me anything." An inadvertent "ooh" escaped as I lifted the lid and looked down at a white gold locket etched with a calla lily. "It's beautiful."

"I noticed you stopped wearing your old locket and thought you might want a replacement," said Martine.

"I lost the old one. Thank you so much for this. It means a lot."

I lifted the locket out of its box and showed it to Grant. "Isn't it beautiful?"

Grant nodded, but the look on his face was pained. Worried Amélie and Martine might see his look and be offended, I quickly put the locket away.

"I have a present for you, too," said Grant. "But it's not ready yet. I wasn't expecting to celebrate your birthday early."

I found Grant's hand under the table and squeezed. "Not to worry," I said, leaning in to kiss his cheek. "Just having you here is all the present I need."

With the gift giving finished, everyone set about reading menus. "Order whatever you want. Tonight's my treat," said Albert. He turned to Amélie. "The duck here is positively amazing."

Within a few minutes, we had all made our dinner choices, and no longer occupied, we sat staring at each other. To say it was awkward would be an understatement. Seeing the problem, Albert jumped in. "Martine, your Grams tells me you're a photographer. Grant's also into photography. He's shown me some really beautiful work."

I watched as Grant eyed Martine, deciding whether he wanted to take Albert's bait. Martine smiled at him, and I ever so slightly nudged his foot. *Please like her. Please be nice.* "What's your favorite subject matter?" he finally asked.

"Faces," said Martine. "What about you?"

"I don't really have a specialty. Not yet, anyway. I go into DC a lot and walk around looking for interesting things to shoot."

Martine brought out her smartphone and waggled it. "Do you have anything with you?"

Grant smiled and dug into his pocket. "Of course."

My heart skipped at seeing his smile. I could see interest in his eyes.

Martine and Grant exchanged phones.

"I got some really beautiful shots of Lex last night you might be interested in," said Martine. "Feel free to email them to yourself if any strike your fancy."

Grant glanced at me, surprised I'd been with Martine before the dance.

I smiled, pleading with him not to make an issue of it. *Please like her. Please be friendly. Please, please, please.*

He rolled his eyes and then turned back to Martine. "Thanks," he said with a half smile before settling back and beginning to peruse. "I'll definitely do that. I didn't take any photos last night, so it would be great to get a few of yours."

I glanced at Albert and was met with a wink. I nodded and smiled back. I had to give it to him. He was a genius. With the briefest of gestures, he'd somehow moved the table toward harmony. Grant and Martine weren't friends yet, but they were sharing something of themselves, a step in the right direction. Albert turned to Amélie and they began to converse, their heads leaning in like old, conspiratorial friends. Wanting to look at Martine's photos, I slid closer to Grant.

Seeing my attention drawn to the screen, Grant flicked backward five images. "I really love this one of you. I've already sent it to myself." Grant held the phone up for Martine to see the one he liked best.

She smiled. "That's my favorite, too. In it, she feels like a mystery to me. Like someone I've never met. I'm fascinated by it."

"Ugh," I said, turning away from the image. I was afraid to look at it and afraid for others to pay it too much attention. In the picture, I was looking for the first time at my newly cropped hair. At seeing myself, my face lit up and I'd smiled.

I'd smiled a smile that was mine, not Alexandra's.

I hadn't intended to, but it had happened. I'd been shocked to see it, and my face brightened even further as if a weight had been lifted. Despite all the years of being Alexandra, there was still some of Milena inside of me. She wasn't totally gone. Martine must have been quick with her trigger finger, because the moment lasted all of two seconds before I brought my emotions back in check.

Wanting to distract Grant from the picture, and seeing another opportunity to insert more of the real me into our relationship this time by building on something I knew Grant liked, I nudged him. "I've always thought night sky photography looked really cool. Maybe we could try that sometime and get our astronomy geek on?" My offer out there, I held my breath as I waited for a response.

Grant flicked his gaze to me, his face all sorts of surprised. He surveyed me then the room, then me again, and I guessed he was trying to figure out if I was joking around with him. I was almost at the point of light-headedness from holding my breath when Grant's two-dimpled smile finally appeared. "That sounds great. I'd love that," he said, leaning over to give me a peck on the cheek. "I'll do some research on it, and then maybe we can try next week?"

Sucking in a discrete breath, I nodded happily as my heart

slowly quieted. Dance shows and astronomy. It was a start, a pretty damn good start. One made even better by the fact Grant and Martine seemed to be doing okay together.

My eyes wandering the table, looking at all the people I was closest to, I was just starting to think the evening might not have been such a bad idea when I heard, "Didn't see that one coming" from Grant.

I leaned back in and found Martine and Sadie on the screen. Kissing. The composition wasn't particularly good, and I guessed Martine had simply held the camera in front of her to snap the shot.

Grant flipped the phone around and held it toward Martine. "Your girlfriend's really cute. You been dating long?"

My heart jumped. I turned to Amélie, praying Albert still had her undivided attention.

I winced at seeing Amélie's eyes narrow. She looked from the phone to Martine and then back again. "*Quoi? Martine tu es lesbienne?*"

Still studying Grant's work and deep in photographer mode, Martine hadn't heard either Grant or Amélie's question. "What?" she asked.

"*Tu es lesbienne? Toi et Sadie êtes en couple?*"

I'd never seen Amélie upset, and it wasn't a pretty sight. Her face was pinched and red. Her mouth stern. Martine looked from Amélie to Grant's outstretched hand.

At realizing what he'd done, Grant jerked the phone to his chest and looked at me wide-eyed. "I wasn't trying to cause trouble," he whispered.

Amélie wiped tears from her eyes. "*Vous n'aviez pas confiance en moi?"*

"Grams, of course I trust you. It's just I didn't want Dad to know."

"Et les soirées pyjama? Vous vous moquiez de moi."

Martine shook her head. "No. No. We weren't laughing at you. Grams, I'm so sorry about the sleepovers."

I looked to Albert for some sort of help but found him stunned into silence, an "oh crap" look on his face. Turning his attention from Amélie and Martine, Grant set the phone down and focused on the napkin in front of him. From the attention he paid it, one might have thought it was the most interesting thing in the world.

Uncomfortable with the dialed-up emotions at the table, I stood. First the homecoming dance and then my birthday—all I wanted was one simple night to be normal without everything going to hell. My abrupt change in position drew everyone's attention, even Amélie and Martine's, who were in the thick of an argument. I'd had no real plan in standing, but knew it was the first step in escaping the situation. I scanned everyone's face in turn, as they looked at me. Albert had gathered my favorite people and had drawn from two worlds to do so. He hadn't realized they were two worlds not meant to collide. "I need to use the ladies' room," I eventually blurted out before vacating the table at high speed. I could feel everyone's eyes on me as I exited. It was definitely shaping up to be a whopper of a birthday. The evening was edging near the backyard carnival on a scale of dreadfulness.

As I followed the signs to the bathroom, I pondered how long I could stay away without appearing rude or having the cavalry charge into the ladies' room. Maybe the stomach flu was in order. Then I could just wrap the evening up quick and go home.

I was reaching for a door marked "Damsels" when a voice came from behind. "Lex," said a rich baritone. "We need to talk."

At the sound of the voice, my heart leapt. In an instant, the downward spiral of my birthday righted itself. I hadn't blown out any candles, but my wish had come true.

Varos.

20

"It's beautiful and so original. I had no idea you could draw," said Martine, as we walked out of Inkology. I'd just spent two hours getting inked, the tattoo a birthday present to myself, and Martine had accompanied me for moral support.

As we faced each other ready to say our good-byes, Martine reached out to touch my bruised cheek and winced. "Let me take care of that real quick," she said, pulling a concealer stick out and beginning to dab my cheek. "Stay still."

I let my eyes wander the street without moving my head. I looked for figures in windows or cars. Was Perun watching? After leaving Martine, I was going to meet Varos, and I couldn't afford a tail.

Martine closed the stick, dropped it back into her purse, and began fishing for something else. "It's not the right color for you, but it looks a bit better." Martine pulled out a little mirror and held it up.

"I know we've already gone over it, but I really am sorry about what happened last night," I said, studying my image. The purple was gone. One cheek was slightly darker than the other, but it didn't look bad, especially with my new hairstyle coming down around my face. "Grant called three times when we got home. He really didn't mean to out you. He feels terrible."

Martine waved away my comment. "Stop apologizing. Grams and I have things sorted. It's fine. I knew she wouldn't care if I was gay. I should have told her. She's got me on dinner and cleaning duty for the week to make up for it. I'm just sorry we got into it at your birthday party."

"Are you kidding? The argument was over when I got back from the restroom. From then on, everyone was all sorts of friendly with each other. What happened while I was gone? I came back and everyone had gone all Stepford."

Martine laughed. "Your grandpa is awesome. He told everyone it was not the time or place for an argument. An eighteenth birthday only rolls around once, so we needed to spank our inner moppets." Martine paused. She looked like she wanted to ask something, but wasn't sure if she should. Finally she spoke. "What the hell is an inner moppet? I mean I get the gist, but still…"

Now it was my turn to laugh. "The line's from Buffy. I watch reruns on Chiller, and Albert has caught a few episodes. It means to get over yourself and just deal. I can't believe he said that."

"Well, I'm glad he did. It gave Grams time to chill out. She wasn't even that mad when we got home. She said Alvin Ailey made her feel mellow."

I rifled in my purse for my keys. "I'm glad she liked it," I said, wishing I'd felt mellow afterward. With my past suddenly colliding with my present at dinner, I hadn't taken in much of the show. I'd been too on edge to really concentrate. My conversation with Varos had lasted less than thirty seconds, just long enough for him to say he'd gotten my message from Okan and seen the webpages, and to schedule a meet. I had so many questions, but he'd answered none of them. "I better get going. Albert's expecting me back home. I have a report to finish by Monday, or I'm going to tank my history grade."

"Are we set for meeting up next weekend at The Gamespot?"

I nodded. "You bet."

Martine and I gave each other a quick hug, then went our separate ways. I had forty-five minutes before the meet with Varos. Although the drive would normally take twenty minutes, I needed at least a half hour to make sure I had no tail. Before leaving the house, I'd checked my car, purse, and clothing with my tracker detector. I was taking every precaution.

From Inkology, I hopped on the highway and sped north then doubled back fifteen minutes later. The highway wasn't particularly crowded on a Sunday, and it was easy for me to keep track of the cars both in front of and behind me. I looked for cars that might be tag-teaming me, but couldn't identify any tails. At the first exit before Fair Valley, I got off and stopped at a gas station. I fueled up my gas hog and watched for any other exiting cars. A caravan with a family of four was the only one to follow me down the ramp. I went inside and paid my hundred bucks, keeping an eye out in case a tail had gone past one exit then doubled back. There was no one. The streets were empty. With gas prices so high, people were driving less.

Hopping back into my truck, I followed the road into Greer, a small town known for quaint B&Bs, a plethora of antique stores, and a thriving foodie scene. I drove down Main Street, took a left near the edge of town, and doubled back on an access road used for shipment deliveries and staff parking.

The meet location was a café in foreclosure. I'd noticed the foreclosure sign and the café's newspapered windows on my drive down Main Street. A Starbucks directly across the street offered a possible reason for the shop's demise. Per standard operating procedure, the café's back door was out of view of Main Street and any prying eyes. I tugged it open and entered. The door creaked ferociously.

Varos popped into view at the sound of my entrance and smiled. "*Priyatno tebya videt'.*"

"It's really good to see you, too," I said, hugging him, then kissing his cheek.

I'd meant the kiss as a simple act of greeting, but when my lips met skin and I felt the warmth of him, memories of the park and the almost-kiss flooded in. Suddenly feeling bashful, I pulled away. "I'm so glad you're okay. Are you sure it wasn't too dangerous contacting me?"

Varos laughed. "Hardly. I know where Okan is, and it's nowhere near here. Come, come. Take a seat."

In the middle of the room was a card table and two folding chairs. I noted a sleeping bag, pillow, and laptop near the far wall. The coffee shop wasn't just our meet venue—it was Varos's temporary safe house. Varos took one chair and gestured for me to sit opposite. A reusable Starbucks travel mug was at my seat.

"A chai latte, no foam. I believe that's your favorite."

"Thanks." I nodded to the sleeping bag. "You using foreclosures a lot?"

"God bless a bad economy."

Although I'd seen Varos the previous night, I gave him the

once-over. "You're certainly looking good these days."

My childhood friend was no longer the pudgy geek I once knew. Instead, he was tan, lean, and had visible muscles. It looked like he'd lost forty or so pounds. The beard was gone, revealing a strong, angular jaw. He'd bleached his hair blond and had let it go shaggy. He looked like a California surfer dude. Ever the Olissan, he wore only a Billabong T-shirt and a pair of battered Levi's, despite the cold weather. Other than his choice of apparel, I was relieved to see nothing about Varos screamed crazy. In fact, he looked healthier than I had ever seen him.

"Physical fitness. It's my new disguise," said Varos, flexing a bicep.

I laughed. "It's working for you."

Varos fished around in his jean's pocket. "I still have this, though." He flipped an inhaler in the air. "I thought it might get better if I got fit, but that hasn't happened. Maybe it's the stress of all this." Varos waved his arms at the barren room.

"Maybe you should retire and find yourself a nice island."

Varos smiled. "Oh, I plan to. Just need to finish a few things first."

Our initial pleasantries over with, Varos and I gazed at each other across the table, a yawning chasm full of questions between us. I'd been joking when I suggested finding an island, but Varos was serious in his reply. Why was he on the run, and what exactly were the things he needed to finish first? Okan had accused Varos of messing with the other cadets, and my stomach did a flip-flop at the thought of my friends being put in danger.

We each had a story to tell, but our new relationship was undefined, our loyalties unknown. We were no longer handler and operative, but nor could we simply be friends, picking up where we left off at Perun.

"Why'd you leave?" I finally asked, starting with the most obvious and least accusing of my questions. Varos had been truly devoted to the movement, and I wanted to know why he'd abandoned it.

For a brief moment, Varos's demeanor went dark, his eyes turning to steel, his jaw clenching, but then he recovered himself, his expression going blank—a tabula rasa. He waved my words away. "Doesn't matter. All that matters is we're both on the outside now. Let's talk about you and what you need. I have a line on a good cobbler in the DC area. I'm thinking three passports should be enough, and I can have them in a couple days."

I tried to interrupt, but Varos continued to talk. I hadn't told him about my change in circumstances. That I no longer needed to run. I'd been too afraid he wouldn't meet me if he knew.

"I have some things I need to do right now, but I'll be able to catch up with you within the next six months, and then we can look for a place to settle." Varos reached across the table and took my hand, running a smooth finger over my knuckles. His eyes found mine.

They were soft.

Open.

Knowing.

Varos understood me in a way no one else could. He knew what it was to be Olissan. To be a spy.

"We'll find a nice island somewhere. Zanzibar's supposed to be pretty great."

I wanted to be mad at Varos for dismissing my question, but I'd seen the darkness in his eyes. It was a darkness that looked a lot like pain. Still, I couldn't let the question go unanswered, not even with his hand now caressing mine, so gentle and soft. I desperately needed some aspect of my life to have clarity. I reached across the table and put my other hand over his. "Why did you leave?"

"Are you coming with me?" asked Varos.

I could see no way around his direct question. Telling a lie had too much chance of backfiring, so I answered with the truth. "I couldn't fulfill the mission they'd tasked me. That's why I tried to contact you. I needed to run, but now I've been taken out of play. I can keep my life as Lex Gastone."

Varos frowned. "It doesn't matter. This is your chance to be free of Perun. You'll get the call eventually. You need to leave now while I can help you. Perun's not what they seem and Al—"

I shook my head, frustrated. "What do you mean by that? What's happened?"

Varos stared at me then abruptly stood, knocking into the table in the process. I grabbed my drink before it could upend. Varos turned away, his hands running through his hair in irritation. "You're still one of them. You're still holding on. You wouldn't be staying otherwise. Lex, I think—"

"You can trust me," I said, walking over and putting a hand on his shoulder. "I won't betray you. Those questions you asked during our last meet…you wanted me to go with you. You wanted to trust me."

For a spy, trust was a four-letter word. With our lives fabricated out of lies, trust was the ultimate form of surrender—we didn't just give it away. I moved to face him, trailing my hand over his arm.

I felt goose bumps rise at my touch.

Surprised by their presence, part of me wanted to pull away, but I was afraid to lose physical contact with him. I was terrified he might bolt. I found his eyes. "I couldn't fulfill my mission because of Albert. He was just a casualty to them but…I love him."

Varos's eyes went wide, and he quickly pulled away. "Lex, you can't love Albert." He shook his head with vehemence.

"What do you mean? Of course I can. It wasn't the plan but—"

"Lex, I think Albert knows about you."

I stepped back, dumbfounded. "What?"

"That tail you had? It wasn't Perun."

"How'd you know about the tail?"

"The house in foreclosure at the dog park? I was using it. I was waiting for a chance to get you out. When I saw the tail, I thought it was Perun, too, but then I investigated. It wasn't them."

"He doesn't know. He can't possibly. He loves me." My voice cracked. "I swear he does." My mind began to rip through my memories of the last seven years. I pulled out the birthdays, the book clubs, the trips. I pulled out the kisses and hugs. The I love you's. He'd said the words. He'd meant the words, I was sure of it.

"Lex, he's pretending. Somehow, he found out, and he's pretending. You're his key to Perun." Varos took my hands and squeezed as if pleading for me to understand.

"Then he would get rid of me," I replied, yanking my hands free, my thoughts returning to the dinner in which Albert had mentioned Perun.

"He's waiting for the right time to turn you and make you his asset. Perun killed his family. He has a reason to keep you close. To play it safe. Think of all you've been able to accomplish because of your feelings for your mother. Because she was taken from you."

Each of Varos's words was like a punch to my stomach. "He loves me," I said. Even to me, my voice sounded weak. "We're going to New Zealand over Christmas. It's a family vacation. I've seen the tickets."

"He doesn't love you. Not if he knows. No one is that forgiving."

"Why'd you leave?" I asked, desperate to get off the subject of Albert. Varos just didn't understand. He'd never met Albert. Albert couldn't know. There had to be another reason for the tail if it wasn't Perun.

Varos looked at me, uncomprehending.

"Why did you leave?" I repeated, nearly choking on the bile rising in my throat. "Why have you been messing with other Perun operatives?"

I glared at Varos, willing him to answer, but he remained infuriatingly mute. My adrenaline surging, it took all my willpower not to grab him and force an answer. Instead, I walked to within inches of his face and locked eyes. "Answer me, goddamnit."

Varos threw up his hands and pushed past me.

"Did Okan say that? Did he tell you I'd been messing with their covers? That's a lie, Lex." Varos turned back to me. "I've been warning people."

"Warning them about what?"

"Do you want to know Perun's big plan for securing independence?" spat Varos, his fists balled tight, ready to strike.

I nodded, reluctantly. Varos's demeanor had shifted sharply. Instead of friendly and calm, he was now agitated and aggressive. I was afraid to say yes, but couldn't say no.

Varos grabbed my drink off the table and sent it flying across the room. It slammed against the wall, splattering brown liquid into a Rorschach. Varos laughed maniacally. "Energy. The need for it rules us all, and they plan to control it. To strangle the world's economies with the need for it. The other cadets are being deployed as economic hit men. They want everyone cowering under their thumb, begging like a junky for a hit."

I winced at Varos's words, at seeing him so close to the edge. Was Okan right? Had living the spy life been too much for him? Had he gone off the deep end?

"How crazy is that?" said Varos, pulling at his hair. "They're after world frickin' domination. It's ridiculous. It's James Bond. The blackouts happening across the United States, those are Perun. They have their hands in all the major world energy markets. Perun doesn't care about Olissan independence. Maybe they once did, but not anymore. There's been a fissure. The people in control of Perun are at war with each other. They're pitting operatives against each other as they scramble for dominance."

Wanting to somehow calm him, I laid a gentle hand on his arm. "What makes you think this? And how could they possibly pull it off?"

Varos grabbed my wrist roughly and stared at me. His face was crimson, his eyes livid. "My parents told me." A single, angry tear rolled down his cheek. "Right before someone at Perun killed them." Varos formed his hand into a gun and brought it to my head, his eyes wild. "Execution style. *Bang, bang.* Dead." Varos pushed his fingers into my head with each bang, as if to drive home his message.

I stepped back from Varos and the pressure of the pretend weapon at my forehead. I was shaking. My heart was sprinting as if a real gun had been pressed to my skull. I could tell my old friend wasn't well.

What I couldn't discern, however, was whether he was wrong.

21

Trying to sort through all Varos had said, I walked back to my truck in a daze, seeing none of the world around me. World domination? A war waging within Perun's ranks? And what of his accusations regarding Albert? Was Albert that good of an actor? Was my love for Albert blinding me to the signs? I had a zillion more questions for Varos after he'd dropped the "world domination" bomb, but he'd refused to talk further, asking me to either commit or leave.

Lost in my own tumultuous thoughts and not in spy mode, I was completely unaware of a figure approaching from behind until a firm hand came to rest on my shoulder. My mind already cluttered with notions of fear and betrayal, I reacted purely on instinct. I spun and threw my hands out hard, shoving the person behind me. Too late, I locked eyes with Grant as he went stumbling backward. An athlete, he quickly recovered himself, but the look on his face was a mixture of both surprise and confusion. "Jeez, Lex."

I shot forward and gave his arm an apologetic squeeze. "I'm so sorry. I was somewhere else. You caught me completely off guard."

"I saw you come out of the old café. What are you doing out this way?"

"What about you? What are you doing over here?" With my mind still reeling, I was stalling. Trying to grasp on to a lie to tell.

Grant held up a smartphone. "Last night when we checked our coats, I put my phone in your purse. I forgot to grab it when we left, so I pinged it with my dad's phone when I couldn't get in touch with you."

"And you came all the way out here to get it?" I asked, trying to control my anger. I don't know who I was more angry at: myself for not thinking to take his phone out—I'd seen it and knew he had the GPS tracker app—or Grant for thinking it was okay to follow me.

"I thought I'd surprise you when I saw you were in Greer. Take you to lunch at the diner down the street. It's a place my mom and I used to go." Grant paused, giving me the once-over. "Now it's your turn," he said. "Why were you in the café?"

"I joined the Virginia Heritage Society," I said with a shrug. "I wanted to pad my college resume a bit more. There's talk of pulling down this block of buildings and putting in a more modern strip mall. We were having a meeting to look at some of the buildings and see if we wanted to proceed with applying for Heritage status."

At the exact moment I finished telling Grant what I thought was a pretty great lie given the circumstances, Varos exited out the back door of the café. Grant turned at the sound of the door slamming shut.

Varos paused at seeing us on the sidewalk, then waved with one hand as he lowered the bill of his baseball cap with the other, shielding his face from view.

Grant followed Varos's departure then turned to me with a look of distrust, his eyes having narrowed, his normally full lips pursed. "Heritage society? I doubt that very much. What's going on? Were you even telling the truth about visiting your parents at the cemetery?" Grant's voice was acerbic, as if daring me not to answer.

"Of course I was telling the truth," I said, my anger rising.

I looked to the sky. Why was this happening now? After talking with Varos, I needed time to think.

Alone.

I turned and gestured for Grant to follow me as I walked to the truck. In no mood for his questions, we walked in silence. I reformulated my lie in my head, and I was about to speak when Grant grabbed my arm, asking me to stop again.

"Don't," I said, jerking free.

"Lex, what's going on with you? You seem so angry."

"Why are you being such a pest?" I shot back.

I look of hurt sprang up on Grant's face, and I immediately regretted my words. I was about to apologize for the second time when his face shifted from hurt to anger.

"Why are you keeping these secrets all of a sudden?" said Grant, balling his hands. "You have a best friend I never even knew existed, and now I find you coming out of a run-down building having just met with some stoner. And then there's the moodiness. One minute you're sweet and loving, and the next you're distracted or depressed." Grant paused to take an exaggerated breath as if calling upon a reserve of patience. "Are you on drugs, Lex? You can tell me if you are. I won't be mad, and I won't tell anyone. I just really want to know what's going on with you."

I gaped at Grant, flabbergasted. Then the word "yes" came out of my mouth followed by a whole new set of lies—a fall during cheerleading at the end of last year, a subsequent addiction to pain medication, attendance at Narcotics Anonymous meetings, and a sponsor—the "stoner" he'd seen exiting the café. I'd told no one. Not even Albert. I didn't want him worrying about me and feared he might not let me go off to college if he knew.

Overcome with emotion at my tale, Grant grabbed me in a hug and began to sway. "Thank you," he said. "Thank you. Thank you. I'm so glad you finally told me the truth. I've been so worried. I love you so much." Grant turned his head to kiss my cheek then nuzzled his face down into my hair, tightening his embrace.

I rested my chin comfortably on his shoulder and relaxed into the feeling of warmth he offered. I was breaking a cardinal rule of Spying 101—keep your lies simple. And I was doing it all to spare Grant's feelings. I was doing it because, even after everything Varos said about Albert and what it might mean, I still wanted my date with Grant under the stars. A picnic blanket, Grant's camera, and us. Me…Milena. I wanted that date to still be a possibility.

I was walking a tight rope, trying to keep my life in balance. Varos would have told me to cut and run. There'd been too many needless lies. Grant was too curious. I was endangering myself. But I couldn't bring myself to sever ties.

I needed to hear his "I love you." I needed to know someone actually meant those words. At that moment, it didn't matter about Grant knowing the real me. I was willing to grab ahold of any affirmations of love on offer, as long as I knew they were spoken honestly.

"Me, too," I whispered into Grant's ear, hugging him tighter. "Me, too."

22

Trembling, I entered Albert's home office. I couldn't get Varos's assertions out of my head. I needed to know the truth about Albert and was willing to scour the house for evidence that might incriminate him. Were there files on me I hadn't discovered? Hidden camera equipment? Bugs?

I walked over to a side cabinet in Albert's office and opened it, revealing the wall safe. At Varos's behest, I'd checked the safe many times but had never found anything of interest. Albert never brought his CIA work home with him. Inside, Albert kept his wife Fern's jewelry along with his passport and some important financial documents. Still, the safe seemed like the first place to start.

It was a keypad entry, and I'd cracked it by simply dusting the keys for fingerprints and then playing with the four numbers that held a print. Albert's combination for the safe hadn't changed in seven years—hardly the actions of a man knowingly sharing his house with a spy. Swinging the safe open, I was surprised to find the velvet cases holding Fern's jewelry were gone. I pulled the folders out and flicked through them, just to make sure there wasn't anything new. Finding nothing, I moved on.

I opened Albert's desk drawers next, starting with the deeper drawer at the bottom. As expected, I found it full of hanging folders containing monthly bills and mechanical servicing info for the Jaguar. Closing it, I shifted to the middle drawer and then the top.

Nada. Zip. Zero.

I moved to the bookcases and began pulling out books one by one and holding them open to see if anything would fall out. Again, nothing.

Feeling slightly reassured, I went upstairs to Albert's bedroom. I checked his mattress looking for seams that shouldn't be there, then under the bed and in his nightstand. In his dresser, I found the usual—socks, undies, and undershirts. Judging from Albert's dearth of socks, I needed to do some laundry. I eyed the bottom drawer of Albert's dresser. Inside were mementos from his marriage. Old love letters, birthday cards, and a photo album with pictures from a beach vacation he'd taken with Fern—a nude beach vacation. I'd nearly keeled over from embarrassment at discovering the au naturel photographs at age eleven.

I opened the drawer and shuffled the contents around, looking for anything out of place. Finding nothing, I moved to the closet. I picked through Albert's clothes, checking pant and jacket pockets for hidden memory sticks. I even inspected his shoes. I ran my hand between each layer of Albert's folded clothes and dug around inside a wooden box he used for his cuff links and watches. I knocked on the closet walls looking for hollow points and hidden enclosures I might have missed during earlier searches. Finally, I rifled through the pile of dirty laundry on the floor, a pile Albert should have brought down to the laundry room. Finding nothing hidden, I scooped it up to take downstairs.

As I passed Albert's dresser, a thought crossed my mind, and an imaginary cartoon light bulb popped up over my head. Where did I hide things I didn't want Albert to see? I hid them under what most embarrassed him—feminine hygiene products. I dropped the laundry and walked back to Albert's dresser, my movements slow. Reluctant. I pulled open the drawer with the mementos and took out the album, running a tentative hand over its smooth surface. The album was big and wide, twelve by twelve inches. Big enough to hide your standard office folders from view.

I began turning the album pages, moving quickly past the au naturel photos but then slowing once Albert and Fern were clothed. I stopped at the photo of Albert cradling his son, Gregory. At seeing it, Varos's words echoed in my head. *Perun killed his family. He has a reason to keep you close. To play it safe.*

I turned the pages, already knowing what would come next— Greg's first birthday party, Greg with spaghetti in his hair, Greg at bath time. As I looked at Greg being taught to ride a bike and Albert's arms raised in triumph when he finally took off on his own, I began to feel Varos's accusations could be true. Family is what haunts and guides us. It can motivate us beyond measure. I thought of all I'd endured because of my mother's death. Because I wanted to protect Olissa and keep others from losing loved ones, from feeling the ache of a loss that shouldn't have happened. My mother was healthy. Decades were stolen from her. Stolen from me.

Family is what could motivate a man to knowingly house a spy. It could give him the fortitude to look her in the eye and pretend he cared. Pretend he loved her. When I reached the last page of the album and turned it to find two well-worn folders tucked in behind, I wasn't surprised.

Pulling the folders out, I opened the first with a clammy hand. My own picture greeted me. A night shot. I was in my pajamas beside the trash can, the vial of poison in my hand. My heart constricted at the sight, my breaths becoming shallow. Although I wasn't surprised by what I found, I was scared by it. My cover was blown. My whole body began to shake, and my ears went dead as adrenaline flooded my system. I began flicking through the photos and documents. Some of the pictures, Albert had taken—me at various sporting events, in front of different monuments during our summer trips, at birthday parties. Others were clearly taken by someone else. Someone who followed me on a regular basis. Someone like the man I'd fought with at the dog park.

"I've known since the beginning," said a voice, startling me.

Albert spoke from the bedroom doorway. It was the second time that day someone had managed to sneak up on me, and I nearly leapt out of my skin at seeing him standing there so casually. "I thought you might need a break from your history paper, so I got ice cream," continued Albert, holding up a plastic bag with two tubs of Ben and Jerry's.

"How?" I asked, managing only a single word.

"You were a mess in the hospital. I don't know what those bastards did to you, but your injuries were bad. You looked like you'd actually been in a car crash. The doctors had you on a lot of pain medication. One night, you started mumbling in your sleep." Albert brought a hand to his neck. "You were wearing Alexandra's gold locket and kept pulling at it. The words were English at first, but then they slid into Oline. My son liked to dabble in obscure languages, so I thought he'd taught you, but then you started swearing and calling the locket a noose." Albert motioned for me to follow him out of the room.

Hugging the folders to my chest, I trailed behind Albert as he went to the kitchen to grab spoons and then to the dining table where he set out the ice cream. We both took a seat and Albert grabbed the tub of Chunky Monkey, leaving me my favorite, Mint Chocolate Cookie. With no appetite, I left it where it sat. I hadn't knowingly spoken Oline in more than a decade, but my native tongue had been what gave me away. I couldn't believe it.

"Lex, there's more than what's in the folder, but that's the gist," said Albert, peeling off his lid.

"Who's been taking these?" I asked, opening the folder. It was second nature for me to scan my surroundings regularly, looking for prying eyes. Missing a tail on a single occasion was one thing, but missing them on several, over a prolonged period of time, was an entirely different story. Either the person following me was a pro, or I'd been careless for years, perhaps enjoying my life as Lex too much.

"A friend."

"A friend?" I narrowed my eyes. "Not an agent?"

"A friend," repeated Albert.

I looked from the folder to Albert. His eyes were still gentle and kind. "Does the CIA know?"

"You were only a child," said Albert before pausing. When he next spoke, his words had gained strength and volume. "No. No, I didn't tell work my orphaned granddaughter was really an Olissan sleeper agent. I know what they would have done to you, child or not."

My mind spun. Had he really not told them, and if so, what did that mean? Did it mean I could stay? That he actually did care? "Why protect me?"

Albert grabbed his ice cream and moved around the table to sit next to me, his eyes on me the whole time. His face was intense, although I couldn't interpret the exact emotion. I sat stiffly in my chair, my hands knotted over the open folder. Albert leaned in and took one of my hands into his.

"You were a lost little girl. You cried for your mother in your sleep. I was a broken man who'd just lost his family. Do you remember how I held your hand at the hospital?"

I nodded.

"Lex, your little hand clutched mine for dear life. You needed me. I could tell. I didn't care what they had done to you as far as mental indoctrination or what plan they had for you. I saw you as an abused child. I knew you needed me. And I needed you."

"You hoped to change me? Undo what they had done?" Suddenly, all of Albert's actions made sense. He'd encouraged me to question the world so I would, one day, question Perun.

Albert squeezed my hand. "Yes. And I know I succeeded. You got rid of the poison they gave you."

"And you watched me do it," I said, shaking my head, finally understanding. Luck hadn't saved me—Albert had. "That's why you mentioned Perun that night and why the threat level was increased. You knew I'd have to run. Did you hope I'd confess? Is that why you bought the tickets to New Zealand, as a bribe?" I paused, thinking over all that had happened following my activation. "And the birthday present you gave me, the Glock, it's because you knew."

"The plane tickets were for getting into Princeton. I've been saving that trip for the occasion. I knew you'd get in. And yes, I mentioned Perun because I hoped you might confess. As for your birthday present, what do you get for the spy in your life but one of the best guns on the market? I have to say I've always been rather touched by your dislike for celebrating Alexandra's birthday. It showed your respect for her. That and always wearing her locket."

I touched my neck at his mention of the locket, even though it was bare. I looked to Albert, studying him. He still spoke with such kindness in his voice. Everything he'd said seemed genuine, but he'd managed to fool me for seven years. How many of the words and actions of those seven years had been a lie? Was only a portion of it a lie? Or all of it? Could I still reach Varos and make a run for it? I dropped my gaze from Albert and started shuffling through the folder again, looking at all the pictures.

"Gathering intel on Perun has been my pet project since you came to live with me," said Albert, breaking the silence. "Perhaps you can help me fill in the gaps and identify some of the players? Have you seen other cadets in the media over the years? Or in person? Do you have a handler? I was planning to tell you the truth and show you those folders. I pulled them from my safety deposit box a few days ago."

I looked up, "You were going to tell me?"

Albert nodded. "I was."

"Because you want me to help you."

"Yes, and because it was time for us both to lay our cards on the table."

I wanted so much to believe Albert and to stay, but I couldn't do what he was asking. I'd felt confused after choosing to protect Albert, but that didn't equal an idealistic one-eighty. Because of Varos, I was more worried than ever about Perun, but if I helped Albert, I'd be ruining the lives of my friends. I'd be putting people at risk who I knew to be good. People who believed themselves to be selflessly working for the benefit of Olissa.

"Lex?" asked Albert, his voice perplexed.

"It was only because of you," I said, deflating at my words.

"What?"

My eyes continued to rest on the folder. I was afraid to look at Albert. "I got rid of the poison because using it would have destroyed you. They wanted me to take you down. Blame you for the poisoning." I paused, searching for the right words. I started playing with the edge of the folder, bending it back and forth. "But I'm not going to be a double agent. I don't have a side anymore. I won't do their bidding. I won't do anybody's bidding. I don't know who's right. I just know I didn't want you to get hurt." Finally, I found my reserve of gumption and glanced at Albert. "I understand if you want me to leave."

A gaping silence fell on the room. Albert opened his mouth several times to speak, but then shut it again. A range of emotions played out on his face: bewilderment, frustration, anger, and disappointment. It hurt me to watch. All I wanted to see was his love.

Finally, Albert spoke. "If I can't take down Perun, I can't protect you long term. They will ask you to serve again."

Ork entered the dining room and came to my side, sitting at my feet with a heavy sigh. I scratched at his neck with my toe. "I wouldn't blame you if you wanted me gone," I replied, trying to make my voice sound strong. My words were a lie, though. I would blame him. I wanted his love. I'd betrayed Perun for him, for that love. I wanted it to be all that mattered.

Finally, Albert shook his head and shrugged as if helpless. "I don't want that."

"Okay," I said, holding his gaze, making sure he meant his words. My muscles were coiled tight with tension. I wanted so badly for his words to be true.

Albert looked down at his Chunky Monkey. Of all the feelings I'd seen cross his face, disappointment was the one that finally took root. Albert's posture caved just a little bit, and his eyes lost some of their brightness and intensity. He nodded to the folders on the table. "The one you haven't opened. I brought that home for you because I thought you'd want to know."

The folder was thinner than the other one but just as worn at the edges. What did Albert think I would want to know? I pulled out the folder but didn't open it.

The answer presented itself a moment later along with a wave of nausea. "Albert, I'm not sure that's a good idea."

"If not tonight, then sometime. Sometime you'll want to know."

I nodded, my mind too cluttered to speak. I needed space to process what had just happened. My heart wanted to believe Albert and to stay, but my training was telling me to leave. That I wasn't safe.

"Everything needs to remain the status quo. You can't let on things have changed."

I nodded again, my mind fully occupied with evaluating my options.

"That means our trip to Princeton for the football game and

then to New Zealand this Christmas to celebrate you heading off to college."

I stifled a grimace. "You can stop playing the dutiful grand-father, Albert."

Albert stared at me, taken back by my words. He suddenly looked hurt. "Lex, I'm not pretending to be a dutiful grandfather." Albert balled his fists and shook his head. "I'm sorry. I see why you're confused. You've just found out I've been hiding things. Lying by omission. I should have made it clear. I love you, Lex. Don't ever question it. I think of you as a granddaughter, and I want to take you to New Zealand. It'll be our last family trip before you head off to school."

I looked at Albert and there it was. Family.

"And Lex... Please don't call me Albert. I know we're not biologically related, but maybe you could indulge the wishes of an old man? Call me grandpa."

23

Feeling unsettled by the complete upheaval of my life and not ready to look at Albert's folders, I turned on the shower and stripped. I peeled off the bandage covering the new tattoo between my shoulder blades and swiveled so I could look in the mirror.

The image of two swan heads emerging from a single body—one head white, one black—was beautiful. The heads had separate identities and characters, a difference achieved via small variations in the eyes and beak. The swans were my Odette and Odile—the two sides of my life, the person I was and the person I pretended to be. After Albert's revelations, I realized I wasn't the only one living with duality, and I wondered if he could really love the white swan and the black.

I was both.

Did he sometimes find it hard to look at me because I so closely resembled Alexandra? Was I a constant reminder of the fate that had befallen his family? Or was he able to push all of it aside and just see...me?

Inside the shower, I can't say whether I bathed or shampooed my hair. I think I mainly stood there, letting the water wash down over me. Albert's confession had changed everything. My life as a spy was over no matter what I did next. Although Perun was still in my life, I saw the possibility of greater normality. Knowing I would never work at the CIA and never need leverage over my classmates, I could see more opportunities for a genuine social life. Grant and I could get our astronomy geek on, and it could actually mean something. It could propel us forward, and I might finally feel safe enough to let my guard down with Grant. Maybe I wouldn't head to college a virgin, after all. Maybe without Perun hanging over my head, I could let him in that much. Be that close to him. Sure, I might still have to dig up dirt on my classmates to appease Perun, but I could do so knowing I was essentially out of the game.

Exiting the shower, I found Ork at the bathroom door. He gave me a *ruff* of hello and then came over and licked at the water on my legs. I shooed him away as I grabbed a towel. "Ork, I don't care if a dog's mouth is cleaner than a human's, you're canceling out a shower."

Rebuffed, he headed for his dog bed, circled three times, and curled into a large ball. He eyeballed me and then gave an audible sigh.

I eyed him back as I wrapped the towel around myself and secured it. "Should I look in the folder? What if I don't like what I find?"

I turned on the tap and started to brush my teeth.

Ork's eyes alternated between falling closed and opening with a flick as he fought sleep.

"Am I boring you?" I asked, my mouth full of toothpaste. I turned and spat into the sink. "This is some real telenovela stuff. I'd think you'd show more interest."

I assessed myself in the mirror as I combed my hair. "You're Lex Gastone. You live in Fair Valley, Virginia, with Albert Gastone, your surrogate grandfather. He's disappointed in you, but he also loves you." A smile snuck onto my face. I watched as my eyes, one blue and one gray-green, narrowed into happy slits.

"Orkney, I think I'm going to have a look. There's nothing to be afraid of. Right?"

No reply. Ork was snoring softly on his pillow, the sides of his upper lip vibrating at regular intervals.

"Yeah, you're right. I'm making a big deal out of nothing," I said, shutting off the bathroom light and climbing into bed with the folders. "This isn't anything to lose sleep over."

Still feeling hesitant, I started with the file on me. I shuffled through the photos—there were probably thirty in all—and wondered who had taken the shots Albert hadn't. I felt confident I was well trained in spotting a tail. How often had I been followed and for how long? If they weren't CIA agents as Albert claimed, who could they possibly be? I didn't think a crew of private investigators would have the chops for such a job. Had Albert hired a private contractor in black ops?

The last photo in the file was me, at age eleven in Scotland, holding Ork after he'd been cleared by the vet to travel. I was smiling Alexandra's crooked smile, but my eyes were confused. Although I faced the camera, my eyes peered off to the side as if I was searching for something. My eyebrows were raised, and my forehead was lined with the kind of worry you don't see in an eleven-year-old child. I hadn't posed for a picture in years, and the act felt foreign. I remember being happy in that moment as Ork squiggled and squirmed and licked at my face, but I also remember feeling unprepared for such an emotion. The smile had snuck up on me quite unexpectedly, and I had looked away from the camera fearing what the lens might find—a girl who didn't belong in those shoes.

Behind the photos in the folder was a twenty-page dossier—the life and times of Lex Gastone. Although the tone was formal and stiff, the content was more like a parent's memory book. The majority of the information started at age eleven. There were report card and aptitude test results, a detailed health history, and a list of hobbies. Albert had an extensive outline of my martial arts training, including results from a couple of competitions I'd entered at his request. Albert correctly noted the bouts I'd thrown in order to hide my skill level. Only one of the file's twenty pages contained information about Milena Rokva. He had my birthplace and date, report card results from half a year of first grade, and a sheet of paper with a fuzzy image of me in a tutu, standing in a group of ballerinas. The picture was taken at the year-end party for the under-eight's at my grandmother's ballet academy. Albert must have downloaded it off the internet.

Most of the material in the file was typed and in a standardized format. However, next to the section on my recruitment, I found a handwritten note in Albert's scrawl.

> *For planned strategic insertions, some Perun recruits were forcibly extracted from the general population based on physical attributes.*

Something clicked in my brain at seeing Albert's words—a realization that should have struck me long ago. "Oh God," I said, my heart clenching and skipping several beats.

Ork whimpered and looked up with bleary eyes from his dog

bed. I looked at him, speechless.

"It's Milena or one of the boys. We've no choice," I said, repeating my father's words the day he brought me to Perun.

Ork stood and wandered over to me, hopping up onto the bed.

I snagged the photo of a young Alexandra Gastone off my nightstand and then dug around in the folder for the picture of me as a ballerina. Finding it, I put the two side by side.

"It's too grainy," I said to Ork, flicking my ballet photo away. "I need something clearer." Ork was sitting on his haunches, watching me, both his front feet on the other folder Albert had given me. "No more procrastinating," I said, pulling it from underneath his paws.

I opened it and began to quickly flip through the pages. My brain was buzzing. Mistress had called me a "Necessary," and now I finally understood the reason why. The first few items in the folder were typed sheets of what looked to be background information. I shuffled past these in search of pictures. The first pictures I came upon were of my family's passports, my maternal grandmother, Amalya, and my brothers', Grigol and Nikolaz. Nothing for my father. Although part of me wanted to stop and study the photos, I moved onward in the pile. I needed a clearer picture of myself as a child.

My heart both sank and leapt at the next photos I found. They were mug shots of my two brothers, Grigol and Nikolaz, mugshots with NYPD tags. "They're in New York," I said to Ork. "They're less than two hours away."

I studied the photos of my brothers, trying to see past their now thuggish exteriors to the thoughtful and kind-hearted boys I'd known. Much to my sadness, a further perusal of the file suggested the good-natured brothers I remembered were gone. Grigol and Nikolaz were residents at Sing Sing Correctional Facility, convicted for armed robbery. "What the hell are you guys doing? Mom must be rolling over in her grave. And poor grandma, she's all alone."

I wanted to close the folder, afraid of how far my family had fallen, but the need to answer one very important question kept the folder open and me rifling through it. I found my grandmother lived in a one-bedroom basement apartment below a liquor shop in Brooklyn. I also discovered she was still working, despite being in her late seventies. She was a maid at a JFK Airport hotel. In Olissa, she had been a prominent ballet dancer and then a dance teacher at the academy.

Why did you guys come here? Where's Dad? I thumbed through several pages of the file in search of his name, Zakhar Rokva. I found nothing.

I wanted to march back down to the den and ask Albert what he knew of my father, of my family's demise. He had to know something, but the picture I found next stopped me. I don't know how Albert obtained it, but it was a photo of me with my mother taken only a month before her death. I remembered the day. We'd traveled to Olissa's capital, Brune, for the National Singing Festival. In the past, singing had been one way Olissan's defied their occupiers. Few people outside of Olissa know Oline, the national language, so the true feelings of Olissan's could be hidden in common songs. In fact, the arts—literature, painting, even ballet—were a major means by which Olissan's spoke their minds against occupiers. The festival was a way for the country to celebrate that history.

We'd gathered at a local park with extended family from Eastern

Olissa we rarely got to see. In the photo, my mother had lifted me off my feet as I dashed past in pursuit of my cousin. She'd tickled me and then set me on her knee. "Smile for the camera, Milena." I'd giggled and flashed my biggest grin.

I ran a finger over my mother's face as tears began to flow. In the last decade, the only picture I'd seen of her was in death. My memories of her as a living, breathing human being hadn't done her justice. She was beautiful. Vibrant. Whole.

I clutched the picture to my chest.

You understand why I had to do it, Mom, don't you? Why I picked Albert over you? I still love you…

Sniffing, I wiped the tears away with a sleeve and set the photo next to the one of Alexandra Gastone with her parents. I let my eyes float back and forth. In the pictures, we were happy girls—little did we know what was to come. I could see we weren't twins. My nose was bigger and my jaw narrower. Still, we could have easily passed for sisters with our fair skin and brunette hair. And most importantly for Perun, we shared one very important and very uncommon feature, heterochromatic eyes—one blue, one gray-green. Reconstructive surgery coupled with injuries mimicking a car accident could and did take care of the differences between us.

I felt ill. Mistress called me a "Necessary" because I was a necessary part of Perun's plan. They needed someone who looked like me. They needed someone who could replace Alexandra Gastone. Plastic surgery can modify skin and bone but not someone's eyes. Before being told about Alexandra, I'd spent nearly five years believing I would be blinded in one of my eyes in order to achieve an insertion, heterochromia being such a rarity. My father's words had kept me from seeing the obvious. I'd thought I was the child he loved the least. I'd believed he had a choice in which of us he gave to Perun. Although I came to love the Perun ideal and my fellow cadets, I'd never forgiven my father for putting me there. I'd been so scared that first day, and he'd been so cold. When I thought fondly of my family, I never included my father. I'd written him out of my life. To me, he was as dead as my mother. I'd done my father a disservice in hating him, in pretending he was dead. Maybe he'd been just as scared as me that day. Maybe he'd thought of me often over the years, praying I was well. This idea hurt. I'd hardly thought of him at all and never with love in my heart.

I took the picture of Alexandra and her family into my hands. I'd been taken because of my eyes, not in spite of them. I wanted to kick myself for being so stupid, for putting too much emphasis on my father's words. What happened only made sense if Perun first identified Albert as a target and then sought someone who could replace Alexandra. Albert was the perfect target for a sleeper insertion. He worked at the CIA, he was estranged from his son, he hadn't seen his grandchild in years, and neither Tabitha nor Gregory had any other family who would lay claim to an orphan.

I let my fingers slide over the three happy figures. My very existence had doomed them, and that made what happen even harder to bear. They'd been living on borrowed time, their demise in a car crash destined.

Guilt and regret hit me like a tidal wave.

24

I found Mr. Dagby watching the Edunews as I entered his classroom. The school day wouldn't begin for another fifteen minutes, and Mr. Dagby was busy writing notes as he listened to the news segment. He was undoubtedly prepping more insightful questions to ask his classes. Questions designed to engage the sluggish brains of the American youth.

Mr. D looked up when I entered and smiled, then promptly frowned. "Lex, what happened to you? You're black and blue."

I brought a hand to my cheek. In my hurry to get out the door, I'd forgotten concealer. "I had an altercation with the ground."

Dagby reached for the TV remote and pushed the mute button, dropping the room into silence. He then tapped at his hearing aids. "What'd you say?"

"I tripped."

Dagby grimaced. "Oh dear. That was some fall. It looks like you got mugged—"

More like thugged, I thought, pulling the assignment out of my bag and handing it over. I'd been up until two a.m. researching and then finishing the paper, and my brain felt like sludge. It was going to be a long day. I didn't think I could take Dagby's earnest show of concern.

"FDR's polio?" said Dagby, scanning the title and then glancing up at me with a look of mild disappointment. "Only got a couple of those."

Not liking the feel of Dagby's disappointment, I nodded to the television, trying to engage Mr. D in one of the meaningful conversations he liked so much. "So what's Hunter talking about today?"

"The fact that Aroyan and his supporters haven't gone away despite their UN appeal being denied and Kasarian taking office." Dagby ran a hand through his thinning gray hair and sighed. "Then there's the Middle East War. There was another series of bombings last night."

"I'm surprised Kasarian's willing to come over for talks given all that's going on at home."

"Goes to show how important he thinks the US relationship is," said Dagby, turning the TV off mute.

Galen Ostroff appeared on the screen. "The blackouts continued last night as the power grids in Denver, Detroit, and New York City each went down for several hours." I was about to head out when a photo appeared to the right of Galen's head. "Perry Donovan, head of City Energy New York, will be speaking to the public in less than an hour to address what is being done about these blackouts—"

I moved closer to the screen until I was right under it. It was the scar through his right eyebrow that sparked my recognition, a backward *C*. It belonged to my old friend, Maxim.

Varos's assertions played through my mind. *The need for energy rules us. They want everyone begging like a junky for a hit. The cadets are acting as...economic hit men.*

Varos may have been a little bit crazy, but it didn't look like he was wrong. Bile crept up my throat, and I had to swallow it back. To Dagby I remained silent, but inside I screamed. Loud and long. *NO. NO. NO. NO. IT'S NOT TRUE. NOOOOOOOOOOO.* But the proof was staring me in the face. I looked away, not wanting to see it. I wanted to crawl under one of the desks, slam my eyes shut, and hide there so I couldn't see it. Who was Perun? Had I been duped by a bunch of crazies? Was Perun responsible for all the US companies in Olissa getting busted? Did they have their hand in everything? Was everything I'd done in service to them… for nothing?

"Ah, Alexandra. Glad I found you," said a voice behind me.

Startled, I whipped around. The expansive form of Principal Quigley stood in the doorway. I blinked, trying to focus through the tumult raging in my head.

Seven years living another life and for what?

"I was just going to your first period class. Can you come down to my office for a minute?" Quigley looked me up and down with a frown on his face. "And maybe you can tell me about what happened to your face along the way?"

Slingshotting into the present, my stomach dropped. If Quigley had somehow found out about my skip days, I'd get detention. And I didn't have time for detention.

"Sure," I said, trying not to sound alarmed. I didn't want to look guilty.

For a short, corpulent man, Principal Quigley walked at a fast clip. I followed a step behind and fiddled with my bag to avoid conversation. I did not need this, not with everything else going on.

My phone chirped with a text just as we neared the front office.

Without turning around, Principal Quigley reached a hand behind him. "Phones should be deactivated at school. You know the rules, Alexandra. You can collect the phone at the end of the day."

"My grandfather wasn't feeling well today," I said, pulling the phone out of my bag and pausing to look at the message. It was from Grant.

It was a short message. Three letters to be exact.

SOS

My throat tightened, and my heart caught at the sight. I quickly pulled up the invitation Grant had sent to connect with his GPS tracker app and hit install.

"Alexandra? Is everything okay?"

Ignoring Quigley, I watched the app load, willing it to move faster. When it finished, I immediately pinged Grant's phone.

"Alexandra?" said Quigley, his voice growing annoyed.

I looked at Quigley and then back to the phone. As I waited for a response from the app, I prayed Grant was bombing a test and wanted to share his dismay as opposed to being maimed by an Olissan thug.

My phone chimed with a response. At seeing the location of Grant's phone, I peeled away from the office and headed for my car. He was at home.

"Alexandra, what are you doing?" said Quigley, following at my heels. "You're not in trouble, I just wanted to talk about the nomination you submitted for Mr. Dagby. For the teaching award. He won!"

"My grandfather is really sick. He needs me," I muttered,

breaking into a jog. I could feel tears welling up in my eyes. Did Okan somehow know I'd misled him regarding Varos? Were they on to me for another reason? They took so many innocents. I couldn't let them take Grant, too. He loved…if not me, then the version of me I'd let him know.

I pulled the keys out of my bag and fumbled with them as I reached the Apache.

"Lex, I can't let you drive upset," said Quigley, coming up behind me, breathing hard. "You might have an accident."

Ignoring Quigley, I unlocked my truck and hopped inside. To my surprise, Principal Quigley reached over me as I was shutting the door and grabbed for my keys.

I seized his hand and spun toward him. "What are you doing? You can't touch students."

Stunned at my anger, Quigley took a step back. At seeing his alarm, I quickly released his hand. I paused for a few seconds to steady myself. At the text from Grant, my system was buzzing with adrenaline. I sucked in one breath, then another, trying to regain my equilibrium.

"I'm fine, Mr. Quigley," I said, my voice measured. "Really, I am. I'm sorry I grabbed your hand like that. My grandfather isn't going to die or anything, he's just sick, and I'd like to be there for him. I promise I'm fine to drive."

With so much adrenaline coursing through me, it was physically painful to sit there rooted in place, talking to Quigley, and then waiting for his reply. Every fiber of my being called for a state of action. As I waited for Quigley to verbally release me, my muscles began to twitch in anticipation. *Come on, come on, come on.* What was probably two or three seconds felt like minutes. I tried to focus on my breath.

Quigley surveyed me, his eyes running the length of my frame then finding my face again.

I smiled. I could see Quigley's expression softening. He wanted to trust me. I'd never caused him trouble before, and he had no reason to doubt my sincerity. But I knew Quigley was the type of man to hem and haw. I envisioned being trapped there for several more minutes as Quigley questioned me, trying to ascertain my fitness to drive, perhaps even calling Albert to check on his status. With valuable time slipping away, I decided not to wait for his permission. I slammed my door and jammed in my key, all while praying my geriatric truck wouldn't pick that moment to fail me.

I caught some shouting and a dumbfounded look as I peeled out of the lot.

25

After circling the border of Grant's property twice and sitting behind a neighbor's bush for what seemed like an eternity, I made my way around to Grant's back door by skirting the hedging his father used as a natural fence.

All the curtains in the house were drawn. During my reconnaissance, I could see nothing inside, which made me exceedingly nervous. The property surrounding the house appeared to be empty, but without high-resolution binoculars, I couldn't be certain given the dense landscaping. According to the GPS tracker, Grant's phone was still inside.

With no intention of going to Grant's unarmed, I'd gone home first. As my adrenaline began to lag, it occurred to me Grant could merely be sick and in need of a nursemaid. Or he could want to talk more about my "drug problem." Grant was that kind of guy.

At my house, I texted him asking for the 4-1-1. I didn't want to go in guns blazing if it wasn't called for. As I typed, I convinced myself Grant's SOS was for something frivolous and non-life threatening.

But then no reply came, and my adrenaline surged once more.

I knew unless Grant needed soup or a chat, I was headed for a potential trap without backup, but I couldn't stand by and do nothing. One way or another, I needed in that house. I pondered calling Albert for a half second, but then decided against it. Although in good shape for a septuagenarian, he wasn't ready for any sort of showdown. And if he called on the CIA for help, it'd be a career ender. I didn't want that for him. They'd find out he knowingly harbored a spy. He'd end up in jail.

Sitting between two hedges, I craned my neck to see around the foliage and looked to both sides to check the backyard for movement. Seeing nothing out of the ordinary, I sprinted to the back door—a door containing a large dog flap used by the previous owner's canine friend. I was willing to head into a potential trap, but I wasn't willing to ring the front bell and announce myself as ripe for the taking.

Before entering, I popped my head through the dog flap and scanned the room. I saw and heard nothing, so I shimmied through, thankful the previous owner's dog was of the large variety.

Regaining my footing, I scanned the room again.

"Grant's not home," said a voice to my left.

I spun, one hand going to my heart, the other going for the Glock nestled reassuringly at my back.

I pulled the gun and pointed, ready to fire.

Mark, Grant's dad, waved me off. He sat on the countertop by the sink, behind the L-bend in the kitchen—invisible to anyone entering through a dog door. "There's no need for that, Alexandra."

I relaxed my finger on the trigger, but kept the gun aimed at Mark's chest.

"Where's Grant? He texted me."

Mark picked up the phone sitting next to him and waggled it.

"The CIA can do all sorts of technological trickery with phones. Things like make a message from my phone look like it's coming from my son's."

"Where's Grant?"

"Penn."

"They called? They're interested?"

"I know some people. He won't get an offer, but he gets the trip. He'll have a few wild parties to remember. Maybe hook up with a girl, someone more appropriate for him. Someone who's not a spy."

"How'd you know?" I asked, still holding my gun high. I was trying to appear calm and collected when, on the inside, I was caving. The walls holding up my life were disintegrating. The CIA knew about me. Not just Albert but the goddamn CIA. I'd been completely and irrevocably found out. Nothing could be the same again. My life as Lex Gastone was over. The only ray of sun slicing through my internal meltdown was Grant's safety.

"Never mind that," said Mark, lowering his eyes to fiddle with the phone. He seemed unconcerned by the gun I held, which could only mean one thing. When his eyes returned to me, he gestured with his head toward a door to my right. "Let's just say we've been watching you for a while."

Out of the corner of my eye, I saw a behemoth of a man walk into the room—six foot seven, crew cut, square jaw. A typical movie henchman.

"What do you want?"

"Your help, of course. I'm going to give you an opportunity to redeem yourself."

My eyes swiveled between Mark and his Goliath. "What makes

you think I would be open to such an opportunity?" Had Albert told them of the poison? Varos's accusations toward Albert replayed in my mind, making it whirl.

Mark didn't answer, but nodded to his man, who took a step toward me.

I turned and fired a warning shot at the big guy's feet—the bullet nicking the tip of his right shoe. This stopped his progression. He turned to Mark wide-eyed. "The little bitch shot me."

"I want to talk to Albert," I said, keeping my gun on the big guy while turning my attention to Mark.

"No can do, kid. It's just you and me." Mark looked to his partner. "And the big baby over there."

I shook my head. "I'm not doing anything without talking to Albert."

Mark gave a nearly imperceptible flick of his finger. "Well then, I guess we're at an impasse."

A second later, I slammed into the kitchen countertop as the behemoth tackled me from the side. The gun fell from my hand at the impact and clattered to the floor.

The giant had my arms pinned. Unable to fight with my hands, I stomped down on my attacker's right foot with a boot heel, then his left, doing a perverse sort of jig on his toes.

On the fifth or sixth stomp, he jerked me away from the countertop and threw me across the kitchen. What little air I had left in my lungs after the first hit vacated when I made contact with the stainless steel door of the refrigerator. I slid to the floor in a messy heap.

I looked up, black creeping in at the edge of my vision. Goliath's attention was on Mark. "You may be paying for my services, but don't disrespect me. If you do, you'll be sorry."

Seeing my opening, I scrambled for the doggy door. I was through it and sprinting for the back fence before Goliath and Mark registered my departure.

"Go get her, you Neanderthal," I heard Mark yell.

A door slammed behind me.

My lungs burned as I struggled to breathe. I tried to kick myself into overdrive. To accelerate. To surge forward.

Nothing happened. If anything, my speed waned. My legs felt numb. Pain corkscrewed through my abdomen—a broken rib.

Goliath grabbed me before I reached the fence and hauled me back toward the house. His grip was tight around my stomach, causing a white-hot pain to envelop my body, attacking every nerve. Doing my best to ignore it, I grabbed for the knife at my ankle. Thrashing, I made repeated attempts. I came up empty each time. I couldn't get the angle for a clean grab.

Sensing the futility of going for the knife, I kicked out with my legs, bucking upward at intervals. At one point, the back of my head hit hard bone—a chin.

Goliath yowled and tightened his grip.

"For God's sake, she's just a little girl. Subdue the bitch," said Mark.

I attempted to scream in order to draw the neighbors' attention. Mark wouldn't want a scene.

But barely a peep escaped.

No air. No voice.

"Take her down," commanded Mark. "If you can't do it, I will."

I caught a glimpse of Mark coming from the back door toward Goliath and me. He held something in his hand.

As I arched my back, striving for another strike to Goliath's chin, my body suddenly went rigid as I registered the stun gun's jolt. In a bonding moment like no other, Goliath and I shared one hundred and fifty thousand volts—one electrode hitting myself, the other Goliath.

I remember hitting the ground, my body, thankfully, falling on top of Goliath's. But then the lights went out. I think Mark must have come forward and knocked me out.

When I came to, I felt as if I'd just run a marathon. I was laid out on a soft surface and knew I was no longer outside. I guessed I was on the living room sofa, a sofa Grant and I had, in better days, made out on. I kept my eyes closed as Mark was in the room, and I heard the sound of a phone being dialed.

"I got her," said Mark.

A voice responded on the other end.

"She's fine. I told you I wouldn't hurt her."

I strained to hear the voice.

"No, I haven't gotten a chance to. She's unconscious."

The voice ticked up a notch in volume, apparently angry at my unconsciousness. The voice was male.

"Look, Albert, I said she's fine. I'm just calling as a courtesy. We'll see you tomorrow."

My heart sank. I felt no anger, only a chasm of emptiness inside. Albert had betrayed me. All he'd said the night before was a lie. Why had he led me on with the speech? Albert had never been cruel.

Although I wanted to keep feigning unconsciousness, Mark

came over and began a pat down. He started at my feet and quickly relieved me of my knife. Not wanting him to find my phone, I pretended to wake with a start and then swiped his hand away. "Get your hands off me, you perv."

Somewhat to my surprise, Mark actually backed off and retreated to a wingback chair opposite the couch. Perhaps he felt uncomfortable patting down someone so young. Or maybe it was the fact I was still technically his son's girlfriend.

"Where's the big guy?" I asked, surveying the room. I propped a pillow under my arm and leaned into it. My broken rib hurt like hell.

Mark smiled. "He's still outside. Too heavy to move."

I nodded. "So," I said. "Albert is part of this?"

"Things have grown precarious, Lex. There's chatter about Kasarian's visit. About the gala and a hitter in play. Both countries need this visit to go well, especially us. Despite the danger, Kasarian's unwilling to postpone."

"So what do you want from me?"

"I want you at the event. I want you to identify possible strikers—people only you could recognize."

"Why would I be open to such a proposition?" I asked, trying to draw out Albert's part in these spy games. Had he told them I wouldn't help? Had he called Mark in to apply pressure? Was Albert running the show or someone else?

Mark reached over and grabbed a folder off a nearby table. He pulled out a photo and handed it to me. I was in my pajamas next to the trash can, depositing the vial inside. The picture was the same one that had been in Albert's folder.

"I'm not doing anything until I talk to Albert," I said, flicking the photo back at Mark, who attempted to grab it but missed. It slid under his chair. I wanted Albert to have to look me in the eye and tell me why he'd done this.

I knew why he'd done it, though.

He'd done it for family, like I had for my mother. What I didn't know was how I could have possibly missed all his lies. Out of morbid curiosity, I wanted to see Albert speak the truth for once. I wanted to see the difference, to know what I'd missed. My fate was sealed—knowing would mean nothing—but still, I wanted to understand why I'd failed. It's funny what the mind grabs on to when the world comes crashing down.

Mark frowned and rolled his eyes. "Albert's too busy for you right now, but he knows where you are. And someone's looking after Orkney, so you don't have to worry about him." Mark paused, leaning forward. His eyes found and held mine, their intensity drilling into me. "Lex, people's lives are in danger. Quit being such a child. This is some serious shit we're dealing with. I know you don't hold an allegiance with Perun. We tested that vial. It was poison, and you got rid of it. So you're either going to help me, or I'm going to throw you in a cell and conveniently forget where I put you. Which is it?"

26

I agreed to help Mark—though it was clear I had no real choice. Too many people had already died—Alexandra, her parents, the people whose lives the other cadets assumed. I no longer trusted Perun. I worried they were not who I once believed them to be.

From what I'd read of Kasarian, he seemed like a good man. His dedication to his sister Alina seemed genuine, and he'd done a lot for the Olissan rebuild. Although his detractors labeled him a US lapdog, he hadn't stopped his sister from informing on C-Fusion Corp, which suggested to me he had a spine. I didn't want to see either of them hurt, especially not when I could prevent it. But I'd initially balked at helping. Why was that? Was it that the CIA was asking? An agency not known for its high moral character—spying was a dirty business, after all, as evidenced by all of Albert's lies.

Was there anyone left for me to trust? I wasn't even sure I trusted myself and could feel paranoia sinking her angry claws into me. I'd played a part for so long, who was I? A spy? A granddaughter? A high school student? A friend? A liar? A traitor? I was all these people, and the contradictions were starting to rip me apart. The people I could trust, like Grant and Martine, didn't know the real me.

I was being asked to give up one of my family members at the gala, and my heart broke at the thought. I knew the CIA wouldn't be kind to the person captured. The cadets had been my family when I needed one. Perun had done terrible things...but it was comprised of many good people. We'd been part of a cause and had accepted the idea that one man's terrorist was another's freedom fighter. It was about perspective. If the ultimate result was something positive for the Olissan people, we'd thought the ends justified the means. But if Perun was not who they claimed, or was somehow falling apart, then we were being used as pawns in a game that was not of our making, To save one good man, I would have to sacrifice another.

Awake after his jolt, Goliath was now banging on the bathroom door. "You done in there? Come on."

"Just a minute," I called, pulling out my phone. After agreeing to help Mark, I'd feigned nausea and sprinted to the bathroom. I needed to say my good-bye to Grant. Not a field agent, Mark wasn't on the top of his game, which was lucky for me, given my rib. I narrowly made it to the bathroom ahead of Mark and quickly locked the door.

I ran a finger over my phone screen to turn it on, praying it still worked after the jolt. The picture of Grant and me at the dance flashed onto the display. At the top right, I saw I had no bars. I'd expected this. Grant's house was in a dead zone for my carrier, but I could still create texts and have them queued to send when my service returned.

I pulled up Grant's number and typed him a message. I wanted to give him some sort of closure since our relationship was obviously at an end. I was no longer a "normal high school girl."

I don't have a handle on the drugs. Had a relapse.

Going to rehab. Not allowed outside contact.

I paused in my typing, wondering if I should say more.

Goliath gave the door another sharp bang. "What the hell are you doing in there? Getting ready for the prom?"

"It's coming out both ends," I called, then let out a groan for effect. I studied the phone screen, my thumbs hovering over the tiny keyboard.

Goliath jostled the doorknob and cursed me. "Really?"

"My gastrointestinal system doesn't do well with intense situations. You're only making things worse by pressuring me." I groaned again, this time louder. It was easy to make the groans sound real, I just had to bend at the waist and tweak my broken rib.

Deciding the message was rather blunt, I typed a quick—

I'll be thinking of you.

My fingers hungered to lay down more words, to share my real feelings. But those words wouldn't have been fair to Grant.

They were too late.

How did we get to this ending? A stupid, impersonal text. It isn't right.

Still, it was all I had. I queued the message and hoped Grant's father wouldn't be able to intercept and delete it. If he'd somehow mirrored Grant's phone, that was a very real possibility, but one I was willing to risk.

A few months down the line, if I was allowed, I'd call Grant and tell him I was moving on. Perhaps he would have found someone else by then; he certainly deserved someone better than me.

After queuing Grant's message, I stared at my phone, wondering if I should send one to Albert. Was there anything left to say?

Deciding there wasn't, I returned the phone to my pocket then leaned over and flushed the toilet. Goliath started to bang on the door again as I washed my hands and sprayed some air freshener.

Smiling, I opened the door to a very peeved Goliath and patted my stomach. "Sorry."

Goliath grunted, fingering my knife that Mark had given him.

"I suppose you'll be wanting this," I said, pulling out my phone.

Goliath palmed the phone and put it in his pocket. "Nice blade," he said, holding my knife up close to his face as if to watch the light play off the metal.

"Keep it. Something to remember me by."

The edges of Goliath's mouth twitched up. "You did put on quite a good show. I've never seen a little girl fight so well."

"What's your name?" I asked.

"Sam."

"Well, Sam. I'm five foot ten. You, on the other hand, are aberrantly tall. I've also been trained to kill since I was seven."

Sam chuckled and nodded. "Touché." He motioned for us to head toward the stairs. Sam walked a step behind me.

"I'm not going to Langley?"

"Mark wants you here. Where he can keep an eye on you, personally."

"You don't fight like CIA. What brand of mercenary are you? Ravenwood?" I asked, looking back at him over my shoulder.

"And you continue to impress," said Sam with a raised eyebrow and a smirk.

I climbed the stairs. "Apparently, not impressive enough to get the full CIA treatment. They farmed out my capture."

"I don't know anything about that. I just do what I'm told in order to pay the mortgage."

"So, not a man of scruples?"

"Blessedly no," said Sam with a near silent laugh. "I completely lack those."

I paused at the top of the stairs and motioned to my left then my right.

"Mark wants you in his son's room. Take a left. Second door."

I nodded and proceeded down the hall. Although I'd spent a fair amount of time at Grant's house, I'd never been to his room. He'd said his father had a "no girls in the bedroom" rule, and although I honored very few people's privacy, I hadn't disrespected Grant by snooping.

At Grant's door, I paused and turned to Sam.

"I'm going to need to give you a quick pat down, just in case you have anything else on you."

I nodded, parting my legs and holding my hands out to the side.

Sam's search was thorough without being inappropriate. When he was done, he patted my shoulder. "Try to get some rest. Tomorrow will be a busy day. And don't get any ideas about making a run for it. Mark's called in some more people, and they're now positioned outside."

Sam opened the door and gestured for me to go inside.

I entered and let my eyes wander over Grant's private domain. I barely noticed the door as it clicked shut behind me. I'd expected Grant's room to be something typical of a teenage guy. I'd expected posters of sports heroes and rock bands, along with a few of scantily clad models. I'd expected sports trophies on the shelves and manky gym clothes on the floor.

As Grant's dad was hardly ever home, I always wondered why Grant was keen to obey the "no girls" rule, but now the reason was clear. Instead of typical teenage boy posters, Grant's photos adorned the walls in intricate patterns. His walls were a diary of sorts. A place where Grant, the artist, laid himself bare. I was surprised to find myself hurt he hadn't shared this part of himself with me. The irony of having such a feeling was not lost on me, given all the secrets I kept from him.

I swiveled my eyes back and forth over the room. It looked like a room that would belong to a bohemian artist. Grant had old cameras on his desk and in his bookcases. Maybe twenty in all. There were all sorts—nineteenth century wooden view cameras, old analogues, and little cameras from bygone days for which I knew no names.

On Grant's bed, I spotted the only camera of Grant's I'd ever seen, his Canon Digital SLR. Sitting next to it was a little gift bag with multi-colored balloons.

I walked over and checked the gift tag. As I'd suspected, it was my birthday present. I sat down and cradled the little bag. My relationship with Grant was, for all intents and purposes, over. Grant might not want me to have the gift anymore. Yet, I wanted to be Lex Gastone, high school student and girlfriend, for just a few more moments. For all that I'd been told to date Grant, I felt sick at the thought of losing him. Hollow. He was more to me than a mark. Way more. My insides hummed at the thought of his kisses, at the sparks that sometimes flew when I let my guard down. And now he was just gone. Never to be seen again. I'd vowed to put more of the real me into the relationship, but I'd never actually gotten the chance. All I had was a proposed stargazing date that never happened. Now there would always be this big question mark of what there could have been between us. Both he and Albert were stripped from my life in the matter of an hour. Needing a few more minutes to cling to my old life and pretend nothing had changed, I began to dig inside the festive wrapping.

I pulled out a red velvet jewelry box. Although Grant was an old-school boyfriend, opening doors and carrying books, he hadn't given me jewelry. I considered the box for several seconds, letting myself revel in the simple act of opening a gift. When I finally did open the box, I found my locket inside, or rather, Alexandra's locket. My heart quickened at seeing it again. I'd thought it was gone for good. Instead of scuffed and scratched, the gold of the locket was now smooth and polished to shining. It looked beautiful again. I opened it to make sure the pictures of Gregory and Tabitha were still there and found the faded images gone, replaced by the same pictures but with their color intact. Grant must have scanned and photoshopped the originals.

Inside the bag was also a card.

> *Happy Birthday, Lex! I'm sorry I didn't get this to you at your party and I'm sorry having lost it caused you so much stress. I realize I shouldn't have taken it from you. I snatched it from your neck one day when I leaned in for a kiss. How dorky am I that I actually did research on how to be a pickpocket? I*

even practiced on a doll. I thought I was being clever,
but we all know how that usually works out for me!
Please believe my heart was in the right place. I just
wanted to give you something special, and I've never
seen you without the locket, but it looked so beat up.
I wanted it to be beautiful again for you.

Love,
Grant

P.S. The original photos are behind the new pictures.

I leaned back on Grant's pillows, ignoring the pain caused by my broken rib, and played with the locket in my fingers. Although somewhat misguided, it was a wonderful gift. Now that things were over, I wondered why I hadn't let myself appreciate him more. Those periods where I'd distanced myself now seemed like inexcusable lost time. Why hadn't I melted into even more of his kisses? Into all of them? Why hadn't I thanked him more for his rides to school or for offering to carry my books? I turned my head to one of the walls with his photo collages. It held a skyscraper, a tree, and what looked to be a depiction of a lunar eclipse. Why, in my text, had I only said, *"I'll be thinking of you?"* He deserved more than that. I felt more than that. Would it have been so bad for him to hear the words from me just once? Didn't he deserve acknowledgment of the feelings I'd been too much of a coward to convey? With everything crashing down, why was I still so emotionally stunted? If ever there was a time to let go and be real, now was it. I had nothing to lose. With prison ahead of me, all I'd have as the years stretched forward would be my memories of Grant. That, and Albert's betrayal. Wouldn't I want those memories to include me being honest in the end?

And now it was too late. My opportunity was gone, lost amidst the chaos of a life lived but never understood. Now that it was gone, now I finally understood. How unfair that endings always come with such clarity.

For seven years, my mind was rarely at peace, always swirling with analyses, scenarios, and predictions. I'd been playing a role and had missed so many of the moments that make up a life. I'd lived them, yet I'd let them slide by with little acknowledgment because they belonged to Alexandra the impostor. I thought of the photos at the museum—all the unexpected moments captured on film. The fear, love, laughter. I'd lived those moments, but my messed up mind never let me have them to keep.

But I was Alexandra.

I was Milena and Alexandra.

I was Odette and Odile.

We were one.

I'd said before I was both, but in my mind, I was always one, then the other. I hadn't believed Milena and Alexandra could coexist. Perhaps, I believed they tainted each other so I kept them separate, but really they were both there together. Intertwined. Always.

All the moments of the last seven years belonged to me. I should have said the words. I should have given both Grant and myself t hat gift.

I got up and walked over to the skyscraper. It was pieced together from images of different glass façade buildings. Each image was a reflection of something—a mother holding a baby aloft, a statue dripping rain, a tree fighting the wind, a bird surfing the air currents. They all melded together to create the skyscraper—a snapshot of daily life in the guise of a building.

Cursing myself for not having shown greater interest in his photography and for not suggesting night sky photography sooner, I moved to the tree. It was comprised of all macro shots—the veins of a leaf; the stigma, style, and anthers of a flower; a marble; the raised hairs on what looked to be a forearm. I smiled at seeing close-ups of Orkney's eye and his nose among the collage. I peeled the image of Orkney's eye off the wall and turned it over to see if it was named. All the photos Grant had ever shown me had names. Usually amusing ones.

In Grant's neat scrawl was the date, the subject, and the name "Her Only Beholder." I frowned and grabbed the photo of Ork's nose off the wall and flipped it to the back, wondering if its name would also reflect my inability to let people in. The photo's title was "A nose by any other name would still be a brownnoser."

I started to laugh, but stopped as my side squawked. I stuck both photos back onto the wall and moved to the eclipse. As I'd looked at the other collages, I'd seen, out of the corner of my eye, snippets of myself in the eclipse. Looking closer now, I saw that I was the eclipse.

"And you thought he was a simple and sweet boy," I said aloud, as my eyes moved over the eclipse, then flicked back to the skyscraper and tree. "Just simple and sweet."

I'd known Grant was irritated with the walls I sometimes put between us—he'd told me as much—but I'd never expected something like this. In the eclipse, I could feel more than Grant's frustration. The walls between us weren't an irritation but a source of real pain. It was no wonder he'd never shown me more than a few photos. I'd kept so much of myself hidden from him, why wouldn't he keep the most intimate part of himself hidden from me?

The eclipsing portion of the moon was done in photos that were black and white. In these, I was either in shadow or facing away from the camera. Most of the pictures were outside shots. Grant and I had taken several hikes in the area. I remembered him snapping a few photos on these trips, but he'd never made a nuisance of himself or made a big deal about setting up a shot. Still, each of the photos had an interesting angle or caught something in the background that was out of the ordinary—a strange cloud, a creepy tree, a bend in the river.

The photos on the other half of the moon, the light side, were color shots but with a strong washed-out look. Each image had a very defined focal point where the color remained, a point where the eye was immediately drawn. In some, it was my entire face, in a few, my feet or hands, but in most, it was my eyes—one blue, one gray-green.

Noticing one of Martine's photos of me among Grant's collection, I pulled it off the wall and went back to sit on the bed. It was a different one than he'd commented on at my birthday. My face was no longer bright and hopeful. My smile was gone, replaced by a frown. It was probably taken seconds after I realized I needed to put the façade back up. Like so many of the others, Grant had modified the photo to have my eyes as the focal point.

They were the eyes not one in a hundred million people had. The windows to my hell. The reason for my hijacked life.

I turned the photo over to see Grant's title, but found something unexpected:

> *I spy beauty*
> *Eyes spy loss*
> *I spy strength*
> *Eyes spy death*
> *I spy knowledge*
> *Eyes spy danger*
> *I spy potential*
> *Eyes spy distance*
>
> *I spy a lie?*

I leaned back on Grant's pillows and closed my eyes. I could smell the cologne I'd given him on his pillow. I rolled over and buried my face in it, letting the clean, crisp scent wash over me.

He was just a simple and sweet boy. Someone who didn't understand me at all.

27

I gazed at a face in the mirror I hardly recognized. The CIA hair and makeup people had given me a blond wig with spiral curls, a set of brown contact lenses, and a pair of sexy librarian glasses to go along with a scoop neck, emerald green gown. The hair was a lion's mane and easily hid my ear bud. I pulled at one of the curls and watched it spring back. Tonight I was Tara Lowe, wife of Peter Lowe, the new CFO of Genetechnica Corp, an up-and-coming medical technology firm with interests in trade with Olissa. The real Tara and Peter Lowe had conveniently missed their flight to Washington due to car trouble—their two Mercedes had disappeared right out of their locked garage.

In reality, my faux date for the evening was Bradley Thomas, a dark-haired, green-eyed, CIA operative tasked with babysitting me throughout the event.

I opened the bathroom door to find Brad waiting patiently on the other side. Looking quite fine in his tux, I was sure to have the best-looking faux husband at the party. "You ready?" he asked, holding up a shawl.

I turned around and let him place the shawl over my shoulders as I checked I still had Alexandra's locket tucked safely in my cleavage. It was all I had left of my old life.

"As I'll ever be," I said, pulling the shawl forward and wrapping it under my arms. The CIA had made a tactical error in selecting my dress, as it was rather revealing in the back and clearly showed my new tattoo. A tattoo someone in the upper crust of society would be unlikely to put on display at a state dinner. My dressers had to scramble to find a shawl.

"Nice ink," said Brad. "Swan Lake's Odette and Odile?"

"You're very cultured for a CIA operative," I said, turning back around and giving him what I hoped was a confident smile.

Brad laughed. "We're not all uncivilized intrigue junkies. In fact, I'm so civilized, I've arranged a tour of the kitchen. Since you're playing an upstart chef, I thought you'd appreciate that," said Brad with an amused smile. He took my hand and led me through the White House halls toward the kitchen. "All the kitchen staff have been vetted, but that doesn't mean a lot when we're dealing with sleepers. Let me know if you want to talk to or take a closer look at anyone in the kitchen. When we get into the party, they'll be a lot of people standing around and talking. My job is to keep us mobile and out of conversations as we make our way around the room. We want you to get eyes on as many guests as possible before everyone's seated for dinner."

"There's a chance I've never met the hitter. I was only at Perun for five years. And then there's the plastic surgery. I had it, and others will have, too."

"We'll all be keeping our eyes peeled for suspicious activity, don't worry. But you're still one of the best chances we have."

At the entrance to the kitchen, we were met by the White House sous chef, a man by the name of Larry with electric blue eyes, a kind smile, and a balding head.

"What's on the menu tonight?" I asked, shaking his hand.

"Tonight's meal is not your traditional White House State Dinner fare. After the election, a reporter asked Kasarian what he was most looking forward to during his US visit, and he said trying a real American cheeseburger. So that's what he's getting tonight. We're also doing a garden salad with sesame dressing, French fries, onion rings, and Coca-Cola cake for dessert."

"Sounds delicious," I said. "You can't beat a cheeseburger." My stomach rumbled at the smell of cooked beef and onion rings permeating the kitchen. Mark hadn't fed me, and I was starving. "So what does it take to become a White House chef? Are any of the staff new?"

"It takes a lot of luck to get a job in this kitchen. And we don't get much in the way of staff turnover. Everyone working tonight has been here since the president took office six years ago."

As Larry showed Brad and I the various cooking stations, I took note of the kitchen staff. There were only two staff, a man and women, young enough to have spent time with me at Perun. I made a point of asking each of them a question and looking at them square in the eyes. The interactions triggered nothing.

After our tour of the kitchen, Brad led me into the main dining room. It was already full of people schmoozing. I immediately recognized a number of senators and congressmen from seeing their pictures on the news. I scanned the milling crowd for anyone from Perun. I half expected to see Isra, a.k.a. Anna Kincaid, although I prayed I wouldn't. As the fiancé of a senator, it wouldn't be very hard for her to get an invite.

Brad ushered me around the room, his hand at my back. We talked as we walked, trying to look occupied.

"So you enjoy your job?" I asked. Unlike Mark and Albert, who were CIA analysts, Brad oozed covert ops.

Brad spotted an older gentleman with a cane coming in our direction. He swiftly turned us ninety degrees and quickened our pace. "We don't want to get stuck talking to him. Eli Mason is a notorious gabber, and he loves to flirt with the pretty ladies. I've heard he's quite the lecher. And yes, I like my job. It has its perks."

"What are those? Distrust, fear, isolation, an early death?"

Brad guided me toward the drinks table where soda and beer were on offer. The casual US dining theme was apparently extending to the drinks selections, and part of me wondered when they'd bring out the box wine. Brad handed me a can of beer. "There's the intrigue, the excitement, the challenge. There's patriotism."

"It's interesting you said patriotism last." I popped the tab on the beer can and took a swig. "And you know I'm not actually legal to drink?"

"Given your background, I figured you could handle it. Plus, you're practically vibrating with nerves."

"It's not nerves. I've hardly had anything to eat in the last twenty-four hours, and I've slept maybe five hours in the last forty-eight."

Brad grabbed himself a Coke and led me away from the table. "At least I can characterize myself as a patriot."

I turned away and smiled at Eli Mason, who was approaching again. "You're really going to go that route? You're what, early thirties? While you were busy with fraternity keg parties and trying to land a girlfriend who would let you round the bases, I was being indoctrinated into Perun's way of thinking. For five years, they taught me to hate this country. And they taught me how to kill." I waved at Eli and beckoned him toward me as I took another sip of my beer. Brad's words had cut me, and I was feeling churlish. He was right, I wasn't a patriot, not of the United States or Olissa, and the latter pained me greatly. I'd dedicated my life to a cause only to find out I was being used for another end. An end I still didn't understand.

Brad grabbed my shoulder and jerked me around to face him. This rough handling jostled my beer, causing it to spill, and triggered a protest from my broken rib, pain radiating across my abdomen. Brad motioned for Eli to take a hike by waving him off and pretending we were about to have a fight. "Sorry, you're right. That was a cheap shot," said Brad, his words not matching the angry face he had put on for Eli's benefit. Brad snatched a napkin off a nearby table and wiped at my dress.

I swiped it from him. "Hands off."

"Do you see anyone you want to take a closer look at? And don't do that again with Eli."

Glancing around the room, I noticed a woman with beautiful, long blond hair. My heart tightened. "The blond woman by the ice sculptor," I whispered, not wanting to say the words.

"What?"

I reluctantly nodded toward the ice sculptor. "The blond facing away from us."

Brad steered me around several different men who approached. "They should have made you look more frumpy. Every guy without

— 213 —

a woman on his arm wants to talk to you."

I waved my hand at him, flashing the wedding ring. "Maybe you should have bought me a bigger rock, honey. Not everyone got to bring a plus one tonight."

As we closed in on the blond woman, she turned, and I realized with relief it wasn't Isra. Still, the woman reminded me of someone. "That's a beautiful dress," I said, wanting to hear her voice.

"Thank you, darling," drawled the woman. "That's a fine-looking accessory you've got on your arm there." She smiled at Brad.

"I'm a very lucky girl," I said, leading Brad away. I definitely knew the woman, but she wasn't from Perun.

"I've never been compared to a purse before," said Brad.

"Sorry, I didn't recognize her at first." The blonde was Meredith Boone, a country singer and newly acquired piece of arm candy for one of the senators. I started to scan the room again. "I'm not seeing anyone among the US—"

My heart skipped a beat as I caught sight of two new people entering the party. I turned abruptly to face Brad so that my face would be hidden. "Shit."

"What it is? Do you recognize someone?" asked Brad, his voice excited.

"Yeah, my best friend."

"From Perun?"

"No, from now. From this life." I grabbed Brad and led him as far away from Martine as possible. "She said she had a date with her father. I had no idea it was this event. You'd think dinner with two world leaders would merit a mention."

Brad put a reassuring hand on my shoulder. "You look very

different. I'm sure she won't recognize you as long as we keep far enough away. Now, tell me which one she is."

"Black hair. Blue highlights. Awesome black dress."

Brad searched the room until he found her. "All right, this isn't a problem. I'll just keep us away. This room is big. It'll be easy."

I hazarded a glance in Martine's direction and then looked around for a place to hide. "Let's move closer to Kasarian's people. Maybe Perun decided to go a different direction with the hit and will use someone placed close to Kasarian," I said, catching sight of Vladik and Alina. Flanked by an entourage, they were making their way to the opposite end of the room from Martine. Vladik kept a protective hand on Alina's shoulder as they stopped to talk with the other guests along the way. A number of the guests appeared disconcerted by Alina and would cast an eye at her intermittently but never hold eye contact. Whether it was because of the wheel-chair or the scar on her face, I couldn't tell. Vladik seemed keenly aware of those being rude to her, though, and would quickly end the conversation and move on.

"It's a shame what happened to her," said Brad, following my gaze. "She was such a pretty girl."

"Didn't your mom ever teach you that pretty is as pretty does?"

"Jesus, prickly much?" said Brad, raising an eyebrow.

I laughed and took another sip of my beer, looking over my shoulder to make sure Martine was still a good distance away. With almost no food in my stomach, and having had very little sleep, the beer was going straight to my head. "Impending incarceration will do that to a girl."

Brad took my hand and squeezed it. "Trust me, you're going to be just fine."

I smiled at Alina as we neared her party. "*Zdravstvujtye*," I said, offering her my hand. "*Menya zovut Tara.*"

"It's rare I get the first hello," said Alina, taking my hand while glancing up at her brother. "It doesn't pay to be in the presence of such distinguished company all the time."

Vladik laughed as he offered me his hand. I took it but continued to talk with Alina. "Within your field, you're every bit as distinguished as your brother." I would have continued to talk with Alina—I was so taken with her—had Brad not nudged me for my rudeness. I turned my attention to Vladik. "No offense," I said.

Vladik smiled. "None taken. I know who got the brains in the family," he said, squeezing Alina's shoulder affectionately. "You speak Oline?"

"We both speak a tiny bit," said Brad, stepping into the conversation and offering his hand first to Alina then Vladik. "My name is Peter Lowe. It's an honor to meet you both. If you wouldn't mind, I'd like to tell you about my company, Genetechnica. I think you might—"

With Brad occupying the conversation, I could turn my attention to others in their group. They had five people in their entourage. Vladik's wife had stayed in Olissa. She was in the early stages of pregnancy with their third child and hadn't wanted to travel.

By their physical muscularity and sweeping appraisals of the room, two members of the entourage looked to be bodyguards, while the other three appeared to be government aides—they kept tapping information into their smartphones. I studied each of their faces in turn, looking for any points of recognition. Other than one of the aides having eyes similar to Grant, there was nothing there.

As Brad continued to talk, I scanned the room again, hoping for a hit. I was starting to feel anxious. Not only did I not want Kasarian to get hurt, I needed to show the CIA I was a valuable asset. One they wanted to protect from Perun and not permanently dump behind bars. Catching sight of Martine and her father heading in our direction, I tapped Brad's foot with my own to signal we needed to move on. With surprising ease, he extricated himself from the conversation, and we waved our good-byes to Vladik and Alina. "Nothing," I said as we walked away. "None of them are Perun, as far as I can tell."

"Dinner's about to be served. Let's do a quick loop of the room again," said Brad, putting his hand at my back and guiding me forward.

"Do you know Albert Gastone?" I asked, finding a new face and studying it. "I thought I might see him here tonight."

"Only by reputation," said Brad as we rounded a corner.

"So how long has the CIA known about me?" I asked, wondering if it had been for the whole seven years I'd lived with Albert.

Brad glanced at me sideways. "Lex, it's best not to think of that right now. You need to focus."

As we finished our tour, President Claymoure announced dinner was to be served, and the guests began to find their assigned seats. Brad guided me to a table near where Claymoure and Kasarian were seated. Martine was one table over, and I made a point to sit facing away from her with my shawl tugged firmly over my shoulders.

"We've got good seats," I said, as Brad pushed in my chair.

"We're running out of time. Don't let it go to waste," whispered Brad.

Three senators and their wives joined us, including the lovely Meredith Boone. "Well, lookey who we have here," said Meredith, patting Brad's arm. "I didn't catch your names before, sweeties."

Brad removed his arm from her grasp. "Peter, and this is my wife, Tara," said Brad, putting a strong emphasis on the word "wife." He nodded a greeting to the others seated at the table, who responded in kind with their own introductions.

As the wait staff appeared and began to bring out the salads, I studied each of their faces, hoping for some hint of recognition. I was beginning to worry I had never met Kasarian's striker and wondered if I could identify a striker I hadn't met. Would something about their demeanor trigger recognition?

A salad was deposited in front of me. To my right, Brad was still fending off Meredith and was beginning to throw manners to the wind. Grabbing a fork, I looked to Meredith's husband to see what he thought of her behavior and found him firmly engaged in conversation with the other two senators, seemingly oblivious to his wife.

I stabbed a cherry tomato with my fork and popped it into my mouth. Before I even bit into it, the tomato was out of my mouth and in a napkin.

Having seen me out the corners of their eyes, Brad and Meredith both turned, Meredith with a look of horror on her face.

"That's not sesame seed dressing," I said, standing and looking at Kasarian's table. "It's walnut oil."

I was about to call out "stop" when Kasarian began to claw at his neck, then collapsed onto the floor.

"Wait, what?" said Brad, popping up. He grabbed for my arm but came up with only my shawl as I raced for Kasarian's table.

"He has a severe nut allergy," I yelled to Brad. "Does anyone have an EpiPen?" I called out to the room. Fearing some sort of attack, the Secret Service was in the process of whisking an uncooperative President Claymoure to safety, causing many of the guests to stand at the commotion.

"There's one in his side coat pocket," said Alina, toppling out of her wheelchair and grabbing for her brother's pocket. Finding the EpiPen, she jabbed it into Vladik's leg.

Vladik continued to struggle to breathe. His eyes rolled up into the back of his head, and then he passed out. Alina pulled the pen free and looked up at those hovering over her. "Call an ambulance," she cried, bringing a hand to Vladik's cheek. I watched for signs Kasarian was responding to the hit of epinephrine, but found none. Instead, Kasarian remained unconscious. Rocking back and forth, Alina cradled her brother's head, muttering to him in Oline.

"Does anyone have another EpiPen?" I called out to the room. At seeing no improvement in Kasarian, I quickly realized Perun would make sure Kasarian's personal EpiPen delivered a dry hit.

A man in his late forties pushed his way into the center, a pen in his hand. "I have one, but it's not safe to do a double hit. If he has any issues with his heart, it could kill him."

"Lex?" said a confused voice. "Lex Gastone?"

I turned my head away from the voice. Away from Martine. With my back bare, she had seen the tattoo—the swan with two heads, Odette and Odile. It was a tattoo no one else would have.

My stomach plummeted as I snatched the pen from the offering hand and moved to stab it into Kasarian's leg. Alina grabbed my hand.

"The first pen failed," I said, desperate for her to believe me. The more time that passed without receiving the epinephrine, the lower Kasarian's chances of recovery. I tried to jerk my hand free from Alina. When it didn't budge, I grabbed her arm with my free hand. It was then I looked down and saw two bell-shaped scars. One on my own wrist, and the other on Alina's. They were identical in every way, right down to the crooked lean.

I gasped. Alina's story ran through my mind—a helicopter crash, reconstructive surgery, a drastic change in personality, a sudden interest in physics, research into alternative energies. The real Alina was dead. She'd been replaced with... *How could it be? Why would it be?*

Alina must have seen the scars, too, because she found my eyes and then abruptly dropped my hand and my gaze.

Free, I plunged the EpiPen into Kasarian's leg.

Alina dragged herself away from me, her eyes darting about the room.

I watched with horrid fascination, as one blue eye didn't track with the other.

Her left eye was glass.

28

With ambulance sirens blaring in the background, Brad, Mark, and Sam ushered me down a White House hallway.

"You did good," said Brad. "Kasarian's going to be okay."

"How'd you know the first EpiPen failed?" asked Mark.

I rubbed at the scar on my wrist. My mind was still spinning.

"Well?" said Mark.

"Because of his allergy, Kasarian would always have an EpiPen on him. In order to ensure he died from the walnut oil, Perun would have made certain that EpiPen failed," I said, wondering if Alina had known that when she administered the first hit.

"Good call," said Sam, his breath catching.

I looked behind my shoulder as his stomach gurgled loudly. "Are you feeling okay?" I asked.

Sam had turned green. "Yeah. Yeah. I'm fine," he said waving me onward.

"Where are we going? This isn't the way out." I dug the earpiece out of my ear and tried to hand it to Mark.

"Keep that in, please. Your night's not over. The Kasarian family and Olissan government would like to thank you personally for your aid this evening," said Mark, moving past me and opening the door on my right. He gestured for me to enter. As soon as I did so, the door closed.

Alina was seated at a small mahogany table. I walked forward and took a seat opposite. My heart was pounding so loudly it dampened all other sounds. Without any warning, any preparation time, I was in the same room as the girl I pretended to be. It was surreal. My mind tumbled, flipped, whirled. I felt barely coherent as my breathing quickened. How on earth could this be happening? It wasn't fathomable. Yet it was…true. She was here. With me… Looking at me… Opening her mouth to talk to me…

"I wanted to thank you personally for saving my brother. He wanted to thank you himself, but the medics insisted he get checked out at the hospital." As she talked, Alina rubbed at the scar on her wrist.

Looking at her and that scar, I wondered if she had put it together. Did she know who I pretended to be? Had she deduced the whole story from the scar, or had seeing it merely shocked and confused her?

I tapped at my ear to indicate I had an active earpiece.

Alina nodded.

I'd thought Mistress had only meant to break me with the hot poker that day, but now I understood. She was molding me to match the young girl whose life I was to steal, right down to the scars on her skin. In all the videos I'd watched of Alexandra, I'd never seen the scar. She was always in long sleeves.

After Alina's initial greeting, we sat staring at each other, neither knowing what to say. All I could think was *Do you know, do you know, do you know?* Alina was the first to break the silence.

"Vlad wanted you to have this as a thank you," she said, handing me a bronze pendant on a chain. "Our mother gave this to him. It was cast from a nineteenth century wax seal used when the Kasarians last held the Olissan throne."

"Thank you." Our hands touched briefly as I took the necklace from her. "It's beautiful," I said, securing it around my neck.

I undid the clasp of her locket and pulled it out from its hiding place under my dress. I handed it over without saying a word then removed my wig, glasses, and contact lenses. She watched me without blinking, perhaps afraid she would miss something if she dared close her eyes for even a millisecond. When my contacts came out and she could finally see my eyes, she nodded her understanding. She had put it together at seeing our matching scars. I wondered if she remembered the night of the accident, when our eyes, so unique, had met for the first time. Had she always known there was someone out there pretending to be her?

"I've been a fan of yours," I said, nodding to the locket. "The way you turned your life around after the accident. It was amazing." As I spoke, I did some mental math. We were the same age, but three years ago, Alexandra had taken over the life of someone five years her senior. She'd had four years at Compound Perun to learn perfect Oline and be trained. That part was doable, but the age difference between the two girls would have been no small feat to overcome, despite the real Alina looking quite young.

I watched with both pleasure and pain as Alexandra opened her missing locket and looked at the faces of her parents for the first time in seven years. Despite being on the outs with Albert, I was saddened his picture wasn't also inside. She probably didn't even remember him, but he'd spent seven years with me, all in the hopes of one day avenging her death.

"Well, now I'm your biggest fan," said Alexandra, closing the locket and holding it to her chest. "I really do love my...Vlad. He couldn't have been kinder to me after the accident." She paused, locking eyes with me. "I had no idea the EpiPen would fail."

I nodded, believing her.

I ran my fingers over the scar at my wrist, wondering how she'd come to possess it. As if reading my mind, Alina mouthed the word "oven."

Sitting in the same room with the real Alexandra, I had so many other questions I wanted to ask. I wished they could all be answered so easily. *Why was she still alive?* I'd seen the car crash wreckage with my own eyes and knew she wasn't meant to survive, yet here she was in front of me. *Was it her intellect? Her research on cold fusion was groundbreaking. The work of a genius. Was that why she now sat before me? That had to be it. Didn't it?* Perun had pushed me hard academically because they knew Alexandra was smart, but they must not have realized quite how smart.

In a miracle, Alexandra had survived the crash, and Perun hadn't seen fit to get rid of someone with so much potential once they'd learned of her capabilities. Perhaps they had kept her alive initially as an information fail-safe in case they needed to feed me more information about Alexandra's life or maybe Tabitha and Gregory. But then Perun must have recognized she was more than just smart and could be of real long-term use.

"What's your IQ?" I blurted out, trying to understand it all.

I shook my head once the words were out. "I'm sorry, that was terribly rude of me."

The woman across from me smiled. "It's off the charts."

Although finding Alexandra alive was a huge surprise, I could understand Perun's reasoning behind it. What I couldn't understand was why they'd decided to use her as a field agent. Why they'd risk placing such an important asset with an enemy like Kasarian? One slip up, and she'd be dead. Surely another cadet would have been better suited for the job. If only I didn't have the damn earbud in and could ask her. I nodded, wishing I could speak freely. "Must be nice."

"It makes me—what you Americans would say—a hot commod—"

Alexandra broke off and I turned at the sound of the door hinges squealing. I grabbed for the wig and glasses on the table, but it was already too late.

Brad stared at me, dumbfounded at my change in appearance. Without saying a word, he motioned that we needed to leave.

I stood up, moved around the table, and gave Alexandra a hug. I buried my ear with the earpiece against the side of her head. I was finally in the presence of the girl I'd looked in the mirror and posed so many questions to over the years, but once again, she couldn't answer me, and I felt a fury bubbling up inside. Would I ever really understand what I'd been a part of? If only we could talk freely, then maybe, just maybe, Alexandra and I could piece things together enough to understand the moves Perun was making—figure out the endgame. Alexandra's life had been stolen from her, and it felt wrong that all I could offer her before leaving was a warning. "Be careful. You can't trust Perun." ⌐

I wiped tears from my eyes as I exited the room. I felt an odd sort of emotional whiplash. Alexandra was in front of me one minute, then gone the next, and for all that we'd spoken for only minutes, I felt her absence intensely. Brad shut the door behind me then grabbed the wig from my hand and stuck it on my head.

"What the—" I said, batting his hands away.

Brad brought a finger to his mouth to indicate quiet.

Unsure of what was going on, I stood still as he straightened the wig on my head then not so gently dug the earpiece out of my ear. He let it drop to the floor where he smashed it with the heel of his shoe. "Why'd you take all this stuff off?" asked Brad, grabbing the glasses from my hand and trying to shove them on.

I snatched them away as he poked my eye. "She wanted to know who I was, so I told her I was an undercover CIA agent. What's going on? Where's Sam and Mark?"

Brad took my hand and pulled me down the hall. "I didn't hear her ask that."

"Then you must have been distracted. Where's Sam and Mark?"

"They've got a bad case of intestinal distress."

As we moved down the hall, Brad pulled my phone out of his pocket and handed it to me.

"What's going on?" I asked again. "Why are you helping me?"

"Let's just say I know Albert by more than his reputation. He's family to me."

We exited into a parking lot, and Brad had me climb into the back of his car, where I covered myself with a blanket. "Some of those pictures Albert showed you. I took them."

"I heard Albert on the phone with Mark," I said from under the covers.

Brad slammed the back door and got into the front seat. "Albert outed you to Mark three months ago," said Brad, starting the car. "Mark had been closing in on you, and Albert thought he could control the situation more effectively from the inside."

"Closing in on me? How?"

"We're not entirely sure. When he started pulling certain files on Perun, Albert got worried. I think Mark was beginning to suspect Albert, though, when he wouldn't bring you in. And that's why you were kept at Mark's house last night and why he hired a Ravenwood. Albert has a lot of powerful friends."

"How often did you follow me?"

Brad shrugged. "When I was in town. Not all that often, really. Albert didn't think they would use you for anything until you were older. He asked me to do more surveillance when Mark started to act funny. I had to bring in a few of my friends from the private sector to help out. It was my friend Zane you met in the dog park."

Brad slowed as he neared the exit checkpoint then sped up again as he was waved through.

"Where are you taking me?" I asked, peeking my head out from under the covers. "And what happened to Mark and Sam?"

"I spiked their coffee with a hardcore laxative. And Albert's going to meet you at a park nearby."

"And what's going to happen to you?"

"Nothing. Hopefully, I'm going to stay in play. Mark doesn't know of my relationship with Albert. I'll claim to have had the same issue as Mark and Sam. I was the first to head to the bathroom while you were with Alina. I'll say I came back and finding no one, assumed Mark had you in custody. I called my superiors and told them I was headed home sick. If I'm lucky, I'll find a way to blame you for what happened to the three of us."

Brad pulled over and stopped the car. "This is your stop. Give the old man my best."

Pulling off the covers, I sat up and peered out the window at the park, at the freedom I'd thought I lost. I reached for Brad's shoulder, squeezing it. "Thank you."

Without further comment, I stepped out of the car, into the night.

29

Inside the park, I dropped the wig and glasses into a trash can and found a bench not occupied by one of DC's homeless. I took a seat, huddling into the shawl. The night was cloudless and cold. I could see my breath hover in front of my face with each exhale. I looked down at my phone, thankful Brad had retrieved it for me, and checked for messages. Grant had sent me a text.

I opened it and found three words. Three simple words. He had said it twice before, and I hadn't responded in kind. *I love you.*

My chest constricted at seeing the words. Not from fear but from pain. I'd been such a stupid girl. Grant knew me better than I'd ever realized. He saw through my eyes, to the loss, danger, and distance that was a part of me. He knew there was a lie. He didn't know what it was, but he knew it was there. What did it matter that he didn't know my real name or that I was once a dancer? He knew me at my core. Knowing that, I could finally believe his words. He loved me.

I dialed Grant's number, my fingers racing across the keypad. I didn't care Grant's phone might be mirrored and his father might listen in. I needed to speak to Grant. I needed to be honest with him at least once. My heart caught at each ring, hoping Grant would answer. After six rings, his phone went to messages.

"Hi, Grant. It's me," I said, my heart beating fast. "I hope you're having fun at Penn. I'm just calling because…

"I just wanted to say…"

I could see the Washington Monument peeking out through the trees. I studied it, trying to find my words.

"I'm sure you already know…

"Grant, I'm sorry I never said…"

After several more aborted attempts, I finally found my voice. "I got your text. I just wanted to say I love you, too." I paused to let the words sink in. Finally having expressed myself, my heart calmed. "I've loved you for a long time. I'm sorry I never said it before now, and I'm sorry my timing sucks. Take care of yourself…"

I hung up the phone and looked down at my screen. My wallpaper had changed to a photo of Grant from one of our hikes. "I love you."

So intent on looking at the photo, I was startled when my phone began to ring and Martine's picture popped up on the screen. I quickly hit the red button, declining her call. Thirty seconds later, my phoned chimed with an incoming text. Martine again.

Lex, what the HELL is going on?

Feeling sick inside, I deleted the message. I had no answers for her. I couldn't tell her the truth, and I didn't want to lie. I desperately wanted to be done with all the stories. I wanted my stint in rehab to be the last lie I told.

I put the phone facedown in my lap and let my eyes settle on the view of the obelisk. Occasionally, I looked at my watch or fondled Kasarian's pendant, but mostly, I sat motionless. Although cold, it felt good to be still so I could think of everything the night had brought. Albert hadn't betrayed me as I'd feared. I was thrilled by this but also scared. The real Alexandra Gastone was alive. I knew now, without a question, that Albert loved me. It was unequivocal. I didn't know, however, what Alexandra's existence would mean for our relationship. Where would I fit into things? I was the façade, the phony, the front. We didn't share blood. I wasn't his real grand-daughter. I was the stand-in, and the real one was back.

Sometime later, a barking dog brought me out of my meditation. It was a sound I recognized. I stood up and spun in a circle.

Curbside, a short distance across the park, was a Black Toyota Highlander with the head of a Scottish deerhound sticking out the rear window.

"Orkney," I cried, running over. "I didn't think I would ever see you again."

The passenger window rolled down, and Albert smiled at me from inside the car. "Sorry we're late."

I kissed Orkney on the snout then opened the door and got in. There was a steel-sided suitcase sitting on the front seat that I had to move to my lap. "What happened to the Jag?"

Albert rubbed the dashboard affectionately then pulled away from the curb. "I sold the Jag. This girl's a hybrid and infinitely more suitable for what we need to do." He nodded to the suitcase. "I sold off some land and some of Fern's old jewelry. We're all cashed up and ready to roll." Albert did a mock drum roll on the steering wheel. "We'll lay low for a couple of months, and then we'll find a place to settle. Probably in Canada."

"I'll help," I said, knowing I needed to step up to the plate given all Albert had done for me.

"We've got plenty of money. You won't need a job. Not for a long time, anyway."

"No. That's not what I mean. I'll help you with Perun. I'll help you take them down."

Albert looked at me, his eyes gone wide, his forehead lined with heavy creases. "You sure?"

"I am."

For a half hour, I silently gazed out the window as the sites of Washington DC faded in the rearview mirror. I felt heavy with the burden of what needed to be said next. I had a lot to lose and didn't know what my revelations would bring. I wanted to keep the knowledge of Alexandra to myself but knew I couldn't. I owed Albert too much to be so selfish. Even if it meant we would part ways and I would have to go it alone, Albert needed to know the truth. When we picked up Highway 95 going south, I finally found the courage to speak again.

"Albert?" I said, my fingers sliding over the scar at my wrist.

"Lex, we've talked about this. Please call me Gr—"

"Albert," I said, stopping what I couldn't bear to hear. "Alexandra's alive. Your real granddaughter, she's alive."

T.A. Maclagan

Acknowledgements

So many people have helped guide Alexandra into existence. A huge thanks to my agent, Lucy Carson, for believing in Alexandra from the get-go and finding her a home. A massive thank you also needs to go to my editor, Samantha Streger, as well as her amazing team at Full Fathom Five: Theresa Cole, Tara Quigley and Jane Arbogast. Thank you ladies for loving Alexandra and pushing her to the next level.

Thank you, Lucinda Blumenfeld, for guiding me through the daunting world of promotion and marketing and thank you, Fiona Jayde, for giving Alexandra a wonderful cover to go out into the world with.

Many thanks to my early readers who helped shape Alexandra into something far better than what she started out to be: Carol Rinne, Larry Rinne, Alonso Cordoba, Andrew Jack, Melissa Muckart, Dan Parsons, Stacy Schoychid and Kim Raymoure.

Special thanks to my language translators: Meredith Welch Devine and Anne Sourdril for their help with the French as well as Eial Dujovny, Henrika Dujovny, and Oksana Korolchuk for their help with Oline (a.k.a. Russian). Not all of what you helped me with made it into the final novel, but I sincerely appreciate you being there to help prop up my foreign language-deficient brain along the way.

A final thanks to my husband, David, and my son, Zac, for their love and support and for always understanding when dinner wasn't made and the house wasn't clean despite the fact I was home alone all day.

About the Author

T.A. Maclagan is a Kansas girl by birth but now lives in the bush-clad hills of Wellington, New Zealand, with her Kiwi husband, son, and four pampered cats. With a bachelor's degree in biology and a Ph.D. in anthropology, she's studied poison dart frogs in the rainforests of Costa Rica, howler monkeys in Panama, and the very exotic and always elusive American farmer. It was as she was writing her "just the facts" dissertation that T.A. felt the call to pursue something more imaginative and discovered a passion for creative writing. *They Call Me Alexandra Gastone* is her first novel.

Visit T.A. Maclagan on her website,
tamaclaganwriting.wordpress.com

CPSIA information can be obtained at www.ICGtesting.com
Printed in the USA
BVOW08s1915050116

431871BV00001B/6/P